Ugly

Donna Jo Napoli

illustrated by

Lita Judge

HYPERION BOOKS FOR CHILDREN

NEW YORK

Printed in the United States of America

First Edition

1 3 5 7 9 10 8 6 4 2

Library of Congress Cataloging-in-Publication Data on file.

ISBN 0-7868-3753-5

Reinforced binding

Visit www.hyperionbooksforchildren.com

Thanks to Barry, Eva, Nick, Elena, and Robert Furrow, who
plowed through early drafts. Thanks also to Terry Crowley
for pointing me to information on native peoples of Tasmania,
and to Marti Trzepacz for finding me photos of Tasmania to
keep by my side as I wrote. Thanks to Neil Cavanaugh,
Richard Tchen, and Eleanor Salgado's and Mary Reindorp's
fourth-period eighth-grade Language Arts classes at the Strath
Haven Middle School in fall, 2004, who made comments on
later drafts. And thanks to my editors, Namrata Tripathi and
Brenda Bowen, who held my hand through it all.

—DJN

For Rosaria
—DJN

For Dave, Jeff, and Elizabeth
—LJ

CHAPTER ONE

The Egg Problem

"DUD!" shrieked a strange voice.

"Never," said the voice I knew better than any other, the sweetest voice of all, the voice I thought of as Mother. "Don't say such a bad word. Quack quack quack quack. Hatch," she said encouragingly. "Hatch. Hatch."

"See? Not a crack. It's silent as a stone. That's a dud egg. Look at the color. It should be ivory. Or a lovely creamy tan. That's green. Look."

"Of course it's green," said Mother. "You're a freckled duck. I'm a Pacific black duck. All my eggs are milky with a slight tinge. Quack quack quack quack. It's a good egg."

"Milky?" said the freckled duck. "That's not milky green. That's plain green. Look at the empty shells of your other eight ducklings. Just look."

"I have to clean out this nest," said Mother in a distracted tone. "The white inside of the broken shells may catch the eye of a falcon flying overhead. Yes, yes, I'll do that right away. Quack quack quack quack."

"That's not the point," said the freckled duck. "The point is, that egg is darker than your others. Look at it."

"It's the same color as other Pacific black duck eggs in Tasmania. Or, well, close enough. Now and then an egg is darker," said Mother. "So what?"

"So it's a dud. Your other ducklings are wandering in circles. They need you. Eight is enough for a clutch. Too many, in fact. Best to count your blessings and forget your losses," said the freckled duck. "Leave it."

"This egg is just slow," said Mother. "It'll

come. Quack quack quack quack. Hatch. Please hatch. Come on now, hatch."

"Eggs are never slow," said the freckled duck.

"This one is."

"Is this your first clutch?" asked the freckled duck.

"Yes," said Mother.

"I knew it," said the freckled duck. "I've had lots of clutches. Believe me: that egg is a dud. Look at it. Just look."

"Stop telling me to look," said Mother. "I am looking. It's a fine egg."

"No, no," said the freckled duck. "Eggs roll out of us, one per day, but they hatch all at the same time. That's how it is, whether you're a freckled duck or a musk duck or a gray teal or a chestnut teal or . . ."

"This Pacific black duck egg is late," said Mother firmly. I could feel her heat as she settled back on top of me.

"You just won't look at facts," said the freckled duck. "Won't look. Won't look." Her voice faded into the distance. "Dud, dud, dud."

"Peep," came a voice.

"Peep, peep, peep, peep, peep, peep, peep," came seven more voices.

And I knew down to my bones and cartilage and bill and newly formed eyelids: these were the voices of my fellow ducklings. They wanted me to hatch, too.

I concentrated. Hatch, I thought. Hatch. Hatch. The effort wore me out. I fell back asleep inside my cozy shell.

"Quack quack quack quack. Come take these duck-lings for a swim," said Mother.

"Huh?" came a low, reedy voice. "Quek quek quek?"

"You heard me," said Mother. "You can't just stroll on by."

"I don't stroll," said the voice, slightly louder. "I waddle. Especially when I'm molting, like now."

"Well, you can't just waddle on by," said Mother. "You're their father."

"That's what I thought," said Father. "I'm their father."

"So take them swimming."

"But I'm their father," said Father. "Quek quek.

You're their mother. You take them swimming."

"I can't. I'm sitting on the last egg."

"There's one more egg?"

"That's what I said," said Mother.

"But the others hatched days ago. If it doesn't hatch soon, it won't be ready to fly north for the winter."

"It'll hatch soon," said Mother.

"Quek quek," said Father. "Leave it."

"Don't be ridiculous," said Mother. "If you won't take these ducklings swimming, then come sit on this last egg."

"I don't sit on eggs," said Father. "I'm the father. Quek quek quek quek. My job is done the minute you start laying the eggs."

"This family has a problem," said Mother.

"Eggs are your problem," said Father. "Not mine."

"But you're my mate."

"Find yourself another mate," said Father.

"I will," said Mother. "Count on it. I'm no goose. But I won't find someone new till next breeding season. For now, you're it. We have a late egg. So this is your problem, too. Help."

"No," said Father.

"Please, please, please, please, please, please, please, please," came the hopeful voices of my siblings.

"Don't try that on me," said Father. "I'm the father. This is mothers' work."

"Oooh, oooh, oooh, oooh, oooh, oooh, oooh, oooh," came the sad voices of my siblings.

"Don't be dramatic," said Father. "This is how Pacific black ducks are. See you later."

Pathetic "bye"s came from my siblings.

"Quack quack quack quack," said Mother. "Hatch. Please hatch."

I struggled. I really did. I knocked myself out struggling. But it didn't happen.

Something else happened, though. Attached to the outside of my abdomen was a yolk sac. Each day my body absorbed some of the nutrition stored in that yolk. So the sac had been getting smaller and smaller. And that day the remainder of it finally disappeared. I had to rest while my belly closed up.

"Off that egg at last, I see," said the freckled duck. "Come to your senses, have you?"

"I'm just stretching," said Mother.

"What a fool," said the freckled duck. "How much time have you wasted on that dud?"

"It's not a dud," said Mother. "I felt something move inside it just this morning."

"Really?"

"Yes. I rolled it over and something squiggled inside."

"You rolled it over?" said the freckled duck. "What are you, a goose? Ducks don't roll their eggs."

"I rolled this egg," said Mother. "And it squiggled. It's alive."

"Well, then, it's dangerous."

"Dangerous?" said Mother.

"Look at it. It's huge."

"A nice size," said Mother. "I'm sure it holds a strong duckling."

"And I'm sure it holds a stranger."

"Quack quack quack quack," said Mother. "What do you mean?"

"I've been asking around," said the freckled duck. "Birds that nest on the ground have babies that hatch all at once. That's how it is, whether you're a duck or a grebe or a plover or . . ."

7

"We've already had this conversation," said Mother. "And, anyway, you're wrong about grebes. They don't nest on the ground; their nests float in the water."

"Picky, picky," said the freckled duck. "The point is, their eggs all hatch at once. Now, goshawks—they're different. Their eggs hatch at different times. Goshawks, not ducks. And guess what happens if the second goshawk chick hatches when there's no parent around to feed him?"

"I don't like guessing games," said Mother. But she sat down on top of me and wiggled. She wiggled and wiggled, as though she couldn't get comfortable. I could tell she wanted to know. I did, too.

"Tell, tell, tell, tell, tell, tell, tell, tell," said my siblings, obligingly.

"The first chick kills the second one. And probably eats him."

"Ewwwwww!" screamed my siblings, in an uncharacteristic chorus.

"That's ghastly," said Mother. "And unduckling-like. Listen to my other ducklings. They would never eat this last one."

"Never, never, never, never, never, never,

never, never," said my siblings. Oh, I really did like
these fellows.

"Exactly," said the freckled duck. "Ducklings
don't do that. When this egg hatches, the goshawk
that comes out will be gigantic. It'll eat you."

"Yikes!" said my siblings.

I was appalled. I'd never do that.

Mother squirmed on top of me. I longed to
hatch. I longed to tell her I'd never ever do that.

"You can't be right," said Mother at last. "I
counted my eggs every day. There were no extras."

"Count for me. Start at one and keep going."

"One, two, three, many, many, many more, so
many, lots, lots and lots, gobs."

"See?" said the freckled duck. "Just as I sus-
pected. You're a lousy counter. You'd never notice
an extra egg."

Mother squirmed. "How on earth could a
goshawk egg wind up in my nest?"

"You were stretching just a moment ago," said
the freckled duck. "And now and then you go off
to eat."

"But quickly," said Mother. "I'm always quick
about it. My ducklings beg for a long swim, but I

rush them in and out of the water and back to this nest. You can ask them."

"Ask, ask, ask, ask, ask, ask, ask, ask," said my siblings.

"All it takes is a minute," said the freckled duck, "and boom, there's the monster egg."

"Before I leave the nest, I check for predators. Every time. I watch for any little shadow overhead. I'd never get off the nest if there was a goshawk about. Never."

"Never, never, never, never, never, never, never, never," said my siblings, but they didn't sound totally confident.

"You'd better go back to your own nest," said Mother. "A goshawk could lay an egg in yours, you're off it so much."

"A goshawk could never spy my nest," said the freckled duck. "I built it under a bush, not out in the open on a sandy bank, like you. No goshawk will ever eat my eggs."

"That just proves my point," said Mother. "If a goshawk had spied my nest, it would have eaten all my eggs."

Mother was smart.

"Maybe it was a crazy goshawk," said the freckled duck.

"This is not a goshawk egg," said Mother.
"This is a good egg."

"Maybe it's something worse than a goshawk,"
said the freckled duck. "Maybe it's a masked owl."

"No," said Mother. "It's a good egg."

"How do you know?" said the freckled duck.

"How, how, how, how, how, how, how, how?"
asked my siblings.

"I just do," said Mother. "It's a sweet egg."

Oh, I loved my mother.

"But you can't deny it's huge," said the freckled
duck. "I bet it's an emu."

"Emu, emu, emu, emu, emu, emu, emu, emu,"
said my siblings in hushed, confused voices.

"Ridiculous," said Mother.

"I should know," said the freckled duck. "To tell
you the truth, it happened to me once. An emu laid
its egg right in my nest. I wasted a lot of time sitting extra on it. Just like you. Once it hatched, I
urged it along with little murmurs of encourage-
ment. And then it didn't even swim. The stupid
thing."

"Your nest wasn't here on Dove Lake, was it?" said Mother.

"No. It was up on the mainland of Australia."

"You should have stayed there," said Mother, in a voice that bordered on rude.

"I couldn't. There was a drought. So I had to come south. This is the first time I've bred on this lake. I'm a vagrant down here."

"Oh," said Mother, in an apologetic tone. "I hate arid regions myself. Well, anyway, all that explains your mistake. Emus don't live in Tasmania. They never even visit here."

"Then I was right before," said the freckled duck. "It's a goshawk. You know the old saying, 'The only thing worse for a bird than looking after someone else's young is having those young eat your own.' We should all attack the egg before it attacks us."

CHAPTER TWO

Rules

"WAR!" screamed the freckled duck. "Get those miniature bills ready, ducklings. It's time to attack."

"Attack?" said a duckling.

"Tack? Tack? Tack? Tack? Tack? Tack? Tack?" came the other ducklings.

"Ridiculous," said Mother. She'd said the same thing before, strongly. But now her voice was weak. I could tell she wouldn't be able to hold up against that bully freckled duck much longer.

I had to do something. And fast. My down was in. As well as the scales on my legs, and the claws on my toes. My abdomen had closed up. I was set to go. And, since it looked like now or never, I chose now.

I swallowed the bubble of air inside my shell. My first breath. It felt great. "Peep," I called, to let Mother know I was coming.

"Quack quack quack quack," came back excitedly.

"Peep, peep, peep, peep, peep, peep, peep, peep," came the happy voices of my siblings.

Let the pipping start. I pecked and pecked with my bill nail in a nice circle pattern at the blunt end of the egg. This was a tough shell. I chipped harder. Pip pip pip pip pip. For hours.

I could hear the freckled duck come and go several times. She always said the same thing: "When it's out and it causes mayhem, just remember that I recommended attack. Remember remember remember."

Mother never answered her. Nor did my siblings.

I chipped away, hour after hour. Finally, *crack*. I pressed the back of my head against the middle of the circle and pushed with all my might. Off came the top of the egg. I peeked out. "Peep," I said joy-fully.

I blinked at the startling sun. Then I looked around. Eyes, so many eyes, were staring at me anxiously.

"Peep," I said again. I pushed myself up tall through the hole, stretched my sticky wings out into the open air, and stepped neatly from the shell that had been my home for almost a month. How odd it was to feel my full length after being so cramped. How strange to move on my own, with nothing touching me but rays of sunshine. The thrill made me woozy. I wobbled.

"Quack quack," said Mother very slowly. "Quack quack."

"What a big, ugly thing." The freckled duck rose up on her legs and flapped her wings, as if to fan me away. "I told you so. I told you."

"All ducklings are bedraggled when they first hatch." Mother turned her head this way and that, eyeing me from all angles. My siblings craned their necks up at me and did the same. "You just have to look at him the right way," said Mother. "Give him time to dry out, and he'll be fluffy and beautiful like my others."

She was deep glossy brown and as beautiful as her words. I loved her so, so, so much. "Peep," I said gratefully.

"Beautiful? Who are you kidding?" The freckled duck shook her chest, then closed her wings in again. "That thing's as ugly as ugly gets."

Mother suddenly stretched her neck forward and ran at the freckled duck. "Go away! Get out of here!"

The freckled duck raced off. "Remember remember remember," she called.

We clumped together in fright.

Mother gave off the loudest, most raucous quacks I'd heard from her yet. She shook all over.

Then she waddled back to us. "Now, ducklings," she said, "never do what I just did unless . . ."

"Unless, unless, unless, unless, unless, unless, unless, unless, unless . . ." we said.

"Exactly." Mother smoothed her ruffled chest feathers with her bill.

We smoothed the down on our chests, though it wasn't ruffled at all.

"Never attack another duck unless. That's the first rule." She waddled in a circle around us. "Actually, the first rule is: Don't get eaten. The second rule is: Never attack another duck unless." She headed away from the nest.

We followed behind in a straight line, me at the rear. A duckling around the middle of the line looked back at me and blinked several times.

"We are Pacific black ducks," said Mother. "We are peaceable ducks. Gregarious. Good tempered. We grace the waters of Tasmania. You'll see lots of poor behavior in this ducky world. But we don't indulge in it. Got it?"

"Got it, got it, got it, got it, got it, got it, got it, got it," said my siblings.

I stayed silent.

"What about you?" Mother stopped and walked back to me, the rest of the ducklings following her in a loop.

Something in me didn't agree with Mother's words. I could imagine attacking ducks. With or without an "unless." The idea seemed quite natural, in fact. Oh, dear. I must be a bad duck deep inside. Bad, bad duck, I said to myself. But I didn't feel bad. I felt confused. Maybe I should discuss this with Mother. I settled down onto my feet and looked up at Mother, ready to argue.

Her face and slender throat were buff. Her blue-gray bill had a sharp black nail. Two black stripes went from the top of her bill straight up through her eyes, which were liquid brown and fastened on me. My mother was a striking beauty. In that moment my love for her was so great, all I wanted was to obey her. "Got it," I chirped.

The duckling who had blinked at me before, now stretched tall, turned in a circle, and blinked at me again. Her face was pleasant. It radiated goodwill.

Mother turned and we ducklings followed her path exactly, in and out the sedges. "Stay close. That's rule number three."

I genuinely liked that rule. I rushed so fast to catch up to the duckling in front of me, that I fell on top of him.

"Hey," he squawked.

Mother stopped. "Is there a problem?"

"Ugly trampled me," finked the duckling.

Blinky blinked at me in surprise.

Mother clacked her bill. "Remember rule number one. Or was it two? Yes, yes, rule number two."

"Never attack another duck unless," I said obediently. "But I wasn't attacking. I was just staying close."

"Too close," said Tattletale.

"Well, that's that, then. It's over. We are Pacific black ducks. We are peaceable." Mother led us through the grasses. "Buttongrass is good to eat. And that brings us to rule number three."

"You already gave us rule number three," I said helpfully.

"Did I? Well, then, this is rule number three again. Eat greens. You can start with this buttongrass."

I adored that rule instinctively. I snipped off grass and jerked my head backward and shook it into my gullet. It was a bit dry for my taste. But I was hungry. I ate and ate and ate.

"Hey," squawked Tattletale. "Ugly's eating all the buttongrass."

"There's plenty," said Mother. "Spring is plentiful."

"But he eats weird," said Tattletale.

"Weird?" said Mother. "Oh, well, some of us eat weird. The important thing is to eat. Make that a rule." She wended her way slowly in the warming sun. I admired the color of her legs. They were yellowish enough to blend in with the sedges and greenish enough to blend in with the buttongrass. My kind, wise mother was a marvel to behold.

"Rule number three," said Mother. Then she looked at me. I stuck my head under my right wing to hold in the objection. "Or, well, rule number many: Always be ready to dash."

"Dash, dash, dash, dash, dash, dash, dash, dash," said my siblings.

"Dash where?" I asked.

"Under a bush, if there's a shadow overhead. Or into the water, if there's a rustle in the bushes."

I could imagine dashing. But I could also imagine

standing my ground and fighting. Attacking, even. Oh, dear. There was that bad duck feeling again.

Mother led us back onto the mudflats, and I looked with wondrous appreciation at the vast extent of water in front of us.

"This is Dove Lake, my dearest ducklings."

"Doooooove," we sang.

"It's the deepest lake I know of. And the best in the world. Pacific black ducks have been nesting here since the beginning of time. You will build your own nests here in a couple of years, in the shadow of Cradle Mountain."

All this news was welcome. The best lake in the world. And it was ours. The truth of that settled inside my brain like a good memory. I admired the shining blue of the water. I admired the shadow of Cradle Mountain, forming two dark double peaks in that brilliant blue.

Mother waddled over to me and poked me gently with her bill. "Are you ready yet?"

Blinky came up and shyly gave me a little poke, as well.

My down fluffed out, dry as the sedge. I wiggled happily.

Mother looked satisfied. "All right, then. Your lessons about the world can now begin. I will teach you everything." She led us to the edge of the water, then slipped in gracefully. We each slipped in after her, one at a time. As I slipped in, Mother said, "See! You're no emu. Freckled ducks are dumb." She positively beamed at me.

We glided along the edge of the lake.

"Water is a safer place than land." Mother ripped a leaf off an overhanging bush. We ducklings all pulled at the leaves. "But it is not without its dangers."

My siblings instantly huddled together, silent, eyes wide. I clambered onto Mother's back. She shook me off and looked at me askance. I fought the urge to jump back on her.

"As I was saying, there are dangers here. Sometimes from places you'd least expect." Mother swung her neck toward a big duck swimming across the center of the lake. His head was thick and his body was stout. And hanging below his bill was a large black lobe of skin. "That bizarre fellow, for example, is a musk duck. Musk ducks are evil."

A shudder went through us ducklings. I

clambered onto Mother's back again. She shook me off again with a reprimanding quack.

"They stay in the water all day long."

That didn't seem so bad. In fact, the water was a delightful place. I could easily be persuaded to stay here all day long.

"And they float low in the water."

Well, that was a little off. All of us swam high in the water, necks long, heads to the wind.

"They dive deep." Mother paused for effect. "And they enjoy it."

Well, that certainly was odd. I hadn't ever tried to dive, of course. This was my first time even floating. But I knew very well that diving made no sense at all.

"And here's the worst." Mother took a deep breath. All of us ducklings took a deep breath. "They eat fish, which any of you might do in a pinch, especially itty-bitty fish. But they also eat frogs and crabs. And if they catch one alone . . . they'll eat a duckling."

We stared at the musk duck in horrified shock.

"So what are you to do?" asked Mother. She looked across us.

We looked back at her, mute.

"Come on. Remember the rules. Which one is important when it comes to the musk duck?"

"One," said a duckling.

"Two," said another duckling.

"Three," said a third duckling.

"No, three again. Or was it many. Rule many, right?" said a fourth.

"The numbers don't matter. Just tell me the rule."

We ducklings swam around in messy circles, muttering rules to ourselves. Which one mattered when it came to the musk duck?

"Stay close," I blurted out at last.

"Right."

"Right, right, right, right, right, right, right, right," said my siblings.

Blinky gave me an admiring set of rapid blinks.

Mother swam over and put her bill to my ear-hole. "Looks don't matter when your brain is that good."

CHAPTER THREE

Enemies

WE SWAM along, heads erect, from
one feeding area to another. Living in the best lake
in the world was good. Learning about the birds
overhead and the fish underneath and the animals on
the shore was good. Everything was good.

Especially the food. Dove Lake formed a big
soup of insects and mosquito larvae. And the greens
were delicious. I ate aquatic fern fronds and floating
nardoo and duckweed and pondweed and green

algae. But mostly, I enjoyed the underwater grasses. The cutting edges on my bill were perfect for tearing at them. I stuck my head down deep and scissored a little off here, a little off there, oh yes, a little off way over there. Yum. Yum yum.

Whap! Something hit me under the neck and knocked my head clear out of the water. I looked up in dumb surprise, right into Mother's face.

"What were you doing?" Mother snapped her head in worry. "Quack quack quack quack."

"Eating," I said.

"Eating? Your head was underwater for three seconds. No, many seconds. No, so many seconds. Too many seconds. You'll drown."

"It felt okay to me," I said.

"It did? Well . . ." Mother swam in a circle around me. "Quack quack quack quack." She looked at my siblings. They had all stopped eating and were watching closely. "Do you need another rule? How could it be? Ducklings don't need to be told not to drown."

"Drown, drown, drown, drown, drown, drown, drown, drown," said my siblings.

"No, no. Don't drown," said Mother.

"Don't drown, don't drown, don't drown, don't drown, don't drown, don't drown, don't drown, don't drown," said my siblings.

Mother looked at me.

"I won't drown," I said.

"Good. We are dabbling ducks." Mother dipped her head briefly and came up with a bill full of food.

Everyone went back to eating.

I put my head underwater again and snipped off grasses right and left, swallowing occasionally as I went. When I lifted my head, I heard shouts.

"Ugly's doing it again!" Tattletale bobbed his head on the end of his stubby neck. "I counted. It was exactly too many seconds. He's trying to drown."

I looked at Mother. "It felt okay," I said before she could speak.

"It felt okay?" Mother took a deep breath, then let it out noisily. "All right, then. If it felt okay, then it has to be okay. Magnificent lungs, I guess. That's that."

"But look at the mess he made," screamed Tattletale.

It was true. The water around my siblings was clean. But the water around me was full of floating grasses. In my enthusiasm, I'd ripped off more than I could swallow.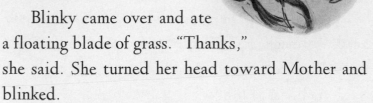

Blinky came over and ate a floating blade of grass. "Thanks," she said. She turned her head toward Mother and blinked.

Mother blinked back. Then she ate a floating blade, too. "Thanks."

The other ducklings now ate up all the floating grass. "Thanks," they said.

Everyone went back to eating. Everyone but Blinky, that is. She glided over beside me. "Watch." And, zip, she upended. Her pale downy bottom glistened smack in front of my startled face. Then, zip, she was upright again, with a bill full of underwater grass. Not a blade floated free. "It's easy. Try it."

I put my head and neck underwater and came up with a full bill.

"That's good." Blinky blinked. "But now try upending."

I swallowed the grass. Then I dunked in my head, my neck, and, finally, the upper half of my body. I righted myself quickly.

"Well?" said Blinky.

"It's awkward. Why would anyone upend when all you have to do is stretch your neck?"

"No one else has a neck as long as yours. Besides," said Blinky, "it's fun."

"Not for me. I don't see the point of upending unless the water's too deep to reach the grasses."

Blinky didn't say anything.

We paddled along quietly, eating. I tried to be neat at first. I really did. But after a while I forgot. It didn't matter, though, because Blinky quickly gobbled my mess. And what she missed, the other ducklings gobbled.

It wasn't long before we met up with another Pacific black duck mother and her string of ducklings. True to Mother's word, my siblings mingled sociably. They were comfortably gregarious. I felt timid, though. I clambered onto Mother's back. She shook me off.

"What is that big, ugly thing?" asked the other mother duck. She and her ducklings gaped at me.

"He's my son." Mother held her head high.

I held my head high, too.

"But he's abominable."

The very word was scary. I clambered onto Mother's back. She shook me off.

One of my brothers tilted his head at me curiously.

"You have to look at him the right way," said Mother. "Besides, he's smart."

"How smart?"

"Very smart."

"He's very ugly compared to my ducklings," said the other mother.

One of her ducklings swam up to a floating log and snipped at it. "Ouch," he said.

"He's brilliant compared to your ducklings," said Mother.

The other duck family swam away. We could hear the mother duck saying, "Don't eat logs. That's a rule. No logs."

Mother led us to another eating spot. "That actually is a good rule, what that other mother said. Never eat a log. Don't even go near logs. Down here in Tasmania, logs are just logs. But when we migrate north to the mainland of Australia, logs can be treacherous."

"What's that mean?" asked Curious.

"They can kill you."

I clambered onto Mother's back. Curious clambered up beside me. She shook us off.

"Logs can turn out to be crocodiles."

"Crocowhats?" asked Curious.

"Just call them crocs. They're the worst beasts of the water."

"No logs," we all peeped in a chorus.

We went back to eating. By this time, the sun was high and hot. I raised one foot backward and sideways, paddling with the other.

"Whoa," said Mother. "What are you doing with that raised leg?"

"Cooling off."

"Raising your leg to cool off? Who ever heard of such a thing?" She swam around in a circle so tight that just watching her made me dizzy. "Staying underwater for too many seconds—I can put up with that so long as you don't drown. Eating messy—that's okay, too, since your siblings benefit. But swimming around with one leg raised—that's downright unducklike. At least for Tasmanian ducks. I don't mind being unusual, but I hate being ridiculous. You'll make us the laughingstock of Dove Lake. Stop it."

I lowered my leg obediently.

Within a matter of minutes, Mother called us together. "Grebes are coming," she said. "Hoary-headed grebes. They aren't ducks. They're different. Just swim on by."

We approached each other silently. I watched the black-and-white father and mother grebe, and their pale gray chicks. All at once the whole family dove. They simply disappeared underwater.

"What happened?" asked Curious.

"Something frightened them." Mother glanced at me, then quickly looked away. "It was nothing. Don't worry about it. Grebes are silly."

They certainly were; from my point of view not much was sillier than diving.

The grebes popped up far from us now and swam away.

"They stayed under a long time," said Tattletale.

"I told you," said Mother. "They're different."

"Ugly stays under that long," said Tattletale.

Mother looked at me with renewed concern.

"But only my head and neck," I said quickly.

"Yes," said Mother decisively. "Magnificent lungs." She went back to eating.

My siblings went back to eating, too.

But I watched the grebes swim in the distance. Mother was right; they certainly were different. They had funny pointed beaks and spiked head feathers. Plus, they were small—hardly more than half the size of us—and, well, the chicks were only a quarter the size of me. And there were only four.

But something about this family felt familiar. And very good. "Oh," I said in a flash of need. "Where's Father?"

"Father?"

"Why isn't he swimming with us? Why isn't he protecting the family?"

"Father's off at the wide end of the lake with the other male Pacific black ducks, naturally. There are lots of birds there. Many kinds. You'll see. As soon as you can fly well, you'll join the males while I go off to molt."

Something inside told me this was all wrong. "But Father should be here, with us, now."

"Don't be ridiculous. I mean, you're a duckling, so of course you're ridiculous. But even a duckling knows better than to ask for his father when he's got a perfectly good mother around." She looked slightly offended.

"You are a perfectly good mother," I said hurriedly. "You're beautiful and wise and kind. You're the best."

"Do you mean that?"

"Yes." I meant it so much, my throat hurt. "The very best."

"Best, best, best, best, best, best, best, best," said my siblings, crowding around.

"Well, then." Mother now looked slightly embarrassed. "Well, well." She upended. When she came right side up again, she busied herself with swallowing a huge clump of grass.

"There it is!" came a loud voice.

I turned. Coming toward us was a strange-looking mother duck. Behind her were other ducks. So many ducks. Pacific black ducks and dreaded musk ducks, and other types I didn't know.

"Gray teals." Mother pointed her bill at a family. I noticed they had a father with them. "Chestnut teals." She pointed again. Another family with the father right there. Oh, I wished our father was here. "Ducks galore!"

"What's with the freaky duckling?" said the mother gray teal at the front of this navy.

"He's not freaky," said Mother.

"He's Ugly," said Tattletale.

"That's just his name," said Blinky. "Really, he's beautiful if you look at him the right way." She blinked at me.

I blinked back.

"Quack quack quack quack." Mother circled us in approval.

"He's hideous," said another mother teal.

"We won't put up with him," said a third teal.

"No one should," said the first mother teal.

One of her ducklings bit me in the neck. It hurt. I bit him back.

He screamed.

Mother swam between us. "What's going on? Biting is bad." She fixed her eyes on me. "Don't you remember rule number two?"

"Never attack another duck unless," I said. "This was a case of unless. He bit me first. That means unless."

Mother looked unsure. "Biting is bad."

"Tell him," I said.

Mother turned to the teal duckling. "Biting is bad."

"Biting is necessary," said the mother teal. "Your duckling must be bitten and struck—in sum, buffeted. Absolutely buffeted."

"But why? He harms no one."

"He's ugly."

"He's a drake." Mother spoke with calm reason,

but I could hear a tremor in her voice. "Looks aren't so important in a male. Besides, he's a genius."

"He's big," said the mother teal.

"He's huge," said the second mother teal.

"He's colossal," said the third.

"Colossal, colossal, colossal," shouted ducklings on all sides.

They attacked en masse. Biting me everywhere.

CHAPTER FOUR

North

I LAY EXHAUSTED and wounded on the mud. Mother sat with her feet tucked under beside me. My siblings clumped nearby, forming a single big ball of down. I longed to be part of that ball, but I could barely move.

For the past week I'd been bitten bloody every day. Mother had tried shifting the hours she took us swimming. Dawn, late morning, high noon, afternoon, dusk, even night. I liked dusk the best. None of it mattered, though. The egrets picked their way past me on their long stilt legs without a second glance. The grebes stopped from the initial shock of seeing me, then they just swam on by. And the swamphens turned tail and hid in the overhanging bushes when they saw me. But the ducks attacked. Always. No matter what time of day or night.

I had tried everything. I looked in the water and compared myself to my siblings. No one thought they were ugly. If only I could have their size and shape and color, no one would think I was ugly, either. No one would attack me. So I hunched down when I swam, to appear smaller. I accordioned my neck, to make it look shorter. I smeared mud across my eyes, to fool others into thinking I had an eye stripe, like my siblings.

But none of it worked. My siblings all looked alike. I was different.

So I tried diving like the musk ducks. If I could dive, I could hide when meanies came. But diving was impossible for me. My body just wouldn't do it. The world was made of dabblers and divers, and I was definitely a dabbler.

Mother sighed now. She opened her mouth as if to speak. Then she shut it again.

I managed to get into a squat position, but I was so tired, I couldn't hold my head up. I stretched out my neck and rested my bill on the ground.

The freckled duck waddled by. Six gray chicks followed her, looking about with that remarkable stupidity of the newly hatched. "See my ducklings. Look at them. Look."

"Very nice," said Mother sadly. "Congratulations."

"Not a single one is ugly. They're better than yours." The freckled duck wagged her tail a few times. "I hear you've been having problems."

"I don't want to talk about it." Mother sighed again.

"I told you." The freckled duck gave one last tail

wag and continued on her way, ducklings in tow. "Remember. I told you."

I remembered. I bet we all did.

No one said anything for a long time.

"I'm hungry," said a duckling at last.

"All we do is race away from other ducks," said another.

"And they catch us anyway," said a third.

"I'm scared all the time," said a fourth.

"Me, too," peeped all the rest of my siblings.

I agreed, but I didn't have the energy to peep.

Mother sighed again. And then again.

"Life is no fun," said Curious.

"The freckled duck is right," said Tattletale. "It's Ugly's fault."

My stomach made a sick flop.

"Ugly, Ugly, Ugly, Ugly, Ugly, Ugly," said six other ducklings.

Only Blinky kept quiet. She blinked at me. Then she peeped softly, "Ugly."

Now my heart flopped, too.

Tattletale waddled over to me. "Go away!"

The seven other ducklings waddled over. "Go, go, go, go, go, go, go!"

Go? Leave my family? The thought was impossible. "I can't," I said weakly.

"Please," came a tired voice. "Please." It was Mother. My beautiful, wise, kind mother.

A lump formed in my throat. I thought I might suffocate—me, of the magnificent lungs. "I can't survive alone," I whispered.

Mother held her head high. "You're my genius. If you use your head, you have a chance. But if you stay here, you have none. The other ducks of Dove Lake will surely kill you."

"No they won't." I worked to lift my own head high. "They don't really hurt me. Not seriously. What's a little down ripped out of my rump? And bruises from bills poking my chest? Nothing."

"You bleed," said Mother.

"Neck nips," I said. "They bleed a lot at first, but they stop quickly. I can survive this, Mother. Really."

"It's going to get worse. The ducks are set against you. You can't stay."

"But, Mother . . ."

"I've made up my mind. That's that. Good-bye, my darling genius." She waddled away. "Come ducklings."

My siblings followed her in a line.

Mother looked back over her shoulder. "Head north," she called to me. She waddled a few more steps. My siblings followed. Mother looked back again. "And make a friend. A friend helps. All anyone really needs is one good friend." They waddled away.

No! I stumbled after them as fast as I could.

Curious was in last place. He turned and snapped his bill in the air toward me. I stopped, in shock. So far as I could tell, in all the beatings I'd taken from the ducks on Dove Lake, no Pacific black duck had bitten me. They'd yanked out down and poked their bills into my tummy, but they left the biting to the teals and the musk ducks. And to me. For I bit back with all the strength I had. I seemed to be the only Pacific black duck who had no aversion to biting. But now my own sibling had threatened to bite me.

Everything was bad.

And getting worse; my family entered the water now. Slip, slip, slip, one after the other. They glided off in the late afternoon sun. They looked peaceful. The nervous twitches that came from checking for other ducks all the time were gone. My family was better off without me. They didn't look back.

I collapsed on the mud.

My head felt like it was filled with muck. I was supposed to follow Mother in a line of ducklings. Nothing else made sense. What was life without a clutch to belong to?

A shadow passed overhead. My heart squeezed tight. I knew I should dash under a bush. But my body couldn't dash anywhere. I was breaking rule number many: Always be ready to dash. Mother would be so disappointed in me.

Luckily, it was a blue-winged parrot. Nothing for a duckling to worry about. The only animals they ate were insects. That shadow carried a message, though: I had to find cover.

I made it over to a close tea-tree thicket and scrambled in underneath. I waited. Evening came and small bats flew jerkily through the dark sky as they ate mosquitoes. Every noise, every movement terrified me.

After a long time, I fell asleep among the whitish blossoms.

Hunger woke me. As usual, sleep had taken the ache out of my body. I waddled quickly through the dark night down to the lake. The water was cool. I drank for a long time. Then I ate and ate and ate. Floating grass blades littered the water around me in every direction. If only my siblings had been here to gobble them up.

And Mother. Oh, Mother.

I wanted to follow her. I needed to follow her.

I swam aimlessly, eating without thought.

A hoot came from the north, where the woods were thick. Then another, a falsetto double-hoot. Could it be an owl? Maybe the Southern Boobook Mother had warned about? But I made out nothing in the black, starry sky.

Still, I moved under the protection of over-hanging branches. The leaves of one gum branch came clear to the water. I swam frantically into the middle of them. Their pungent minty smell enveloped me. Gradually I yielded to sleep again.

Sunlight sparkled off the water. I came out into the open and looked around. It was late afternoon already. Sadness certainly made me sleepy.

A Pacific black duck family was feeding not far away. But it wasn't mine. The chicks were smaller, younger, so young the mother still spouted rules lovingly. I heard her say, "Stay close."

Rule number three. Stay close.

The soundness of that rule pierced my soul. Staying close was right.

Being alone was wrong.

Surely Mother would see it the same way. She taught us that rule, after all. Worry had overcome her and muddied her judgment. She must have changed her mind by now. She must have. I could go back to my family. Oh, rapturous day. I rushed through the waters searching for them, my head as high as I could hold it. Where were they?

The freckled duck and her ducklings loafed on a sand spit. "Looking for something?" called the mother duck.

Well, I wasn't about to ask her for help. I keep moving straight ahead.

"Oh, did your mother finally wise up and abandon you?"

I swam faster.

"Ugly," she spat after me. "Ugly, ugly, ugly!"

There! Yes, oh yes. I saw them: My perfectly good mother and my eight happy siblings. "Family!" I called. "Wait for me. I'm coming. Wait."

Mother glanced at me. My siblings glanced at me. Then they swam fast in the other direction.

"Look. It's that ugly duckling," came a teal voice.

"Get him!" came another.

"Attack!" came the voices of a navy of ducks.

I didn't know which way to go. My family was

fleeing in one direction, and the teals were coming at me from the other. By the time I got the where-withal to head in a third direction, the teals were upon me. They jumped on top of me and held me down, my whole body underwater. This was new. This was not biting and poking. This didn't even hurt. It was just thoroughly nasty.

"It won't be long now," I heard them shouting. "Any second."

Then I got it; they were trying to drown me. It's what Mother had predicted: death by ducks. Murder. I struggled. There were so many of them— so many pairs of webbed feet pushing me down. I struggled like mad.

Then I stopped. I was too ugly to be part of my family. Too ugly to be part of any family. And without a family, what was the point?

I let my body go lax.

The teals left. They simply swam away. What was going on? Had they finally had pity on me?

"Dead," one called out. "Dead duck."

"Dead duck, dead duck, dead duck," sounded over and over.

Oh, of course. They thought I had drowned

already. I'd been underwater for many seconds. Too many seconds for any ordinary Pacific black duck, any duck without magnificent lungs.

But I had magnificent lungs. That's what Mother said. And I was her darling genius.

Darling.

I was darling.

Maybe I wanted to live, after all.

I stayed underwater for as long as I could. When I finally came up, there wasn't a teal in sight. But a family of freckled ducks was coming this way. The mother spotted me. Oh no, it was that same freckled duck again. "The ugly duckling!" she shrieked. Another duck family joined her. And another. They came at me, thrashing across the water in a cloud of spray.

I swam for dear life toward the shore, where a young wallaby leaned over the water, staring down at something. Mother had told us all about wallabies. They didn't harm anyone. And best of all, the wallabies of Tasmania had shaggy fur, much longer than the fur of the bigger wallabies up on the Australian mainland, where the winters were milder. Fur was like grass; it offered someplace to hide. I waddled quick out of the water and clambered onto his back, wiggling to get cover.

"What?" said the wallaby. He straightened tall in confusion. "What?"

The ducks gathered in the water, quacking up a din. "Where'd he go? Where, where, where?"

Mother had told me to use my head and go north and make a friend. That way I'd have a chance. "Go north," I called to the wallaby. After all, my voice was in my head, so using my voice was using my head. I tunneled my way through his fur up to his neck. "North," I said insistently in his ear. "Go north."

The dazed wallaby tilted his head. "North?"

"North?" screamed the freckled duck mother. "North? He went north?"

"How could he go north?" said another duck. "We saw him come this way."

I peeked past the wallaby's neck and watched those ducks swimming past each other in angry circles.

"I think he climbed up the wallaby's back."

"You're mental."

"No, I'm not. Turn around, Wallaby."

"What?" said the wallaby. "Why?"

"North," I said in the wallaby's ear again.

"We want to see if there's a duck on your back," said the mother freckled duck, shaking her head in a frenzy of meanness. "An ugly duck." Her feathers stuck out all cockeyed. "The ugliest duck you ever saw."

"I'm looking at the ugliest duck I ever saw," said the wallaby without rancor.

The freckled duck gasped in shock.

I would have laughed if I wasn't scared out of my wits.

"North," I said again in his ear.

"North," sang the wallaby. And I barely had enough time to clamp my bill onto his fur before we hopped away.

CHAPTER FIVE

Friends

THE WALLABY hopped northward. He was clearly an agreeable sort, the right kind of fellow to be my friend. I was doing exactly what Mother had told me to do. I'd always do exactly what Mother had told me. She was wise; her rules would carry me through.

I held on tight with my bill, and suffered the blows of my body slamming against his shoulder blades every time he landed from a hop. It didn't seem to bother the wallaby at all, which isn't surprising; even though I had grown a lot since hatching, I was still small compared to him. But each blow knocked the air out of me. Wallaby hopping was, unfortunately, nothing like graceful duck gliding.

We traveled past waterfalls and a charming little lake. When we came to the north forest, the wallaby turned right.

Hey, that was the wrong way.

I didn't dare open my bill, or I'd fall off my host. So I battered him with my webbed feet.

He stopped. "Okay, I'm ready. Get off."

"I don't want to get off," I gasped. "I want to go north. You turned the wrong way."

The wallaby hopped around like a crazy thing. I fell off.

"Put up your dukes!" The wallaby came at me with his front paws curled into fists.

"Peep," I said, feeling suddenly like a newly hatched babe in the face of this danger. "Peep peep. What's going on?"

He punched me between the eyes.

I landed on my back and the world swirled around me.

"Get up." The wallaby hopped back and forth.
"Are you going to punch me again?"

"Yes."

"Then I'm not getting up."

"You started it." The wallaby took a few punches at the air. "You wanted to box. I'm always ready for boxing. Come on. Put up your dukes."

"Box?" I said. "Ducks don't box."

"Oh." The wallaby looked disappointed. But he brightened again almost immediately. "Dinner-time."

"Let's go back toward the forest first," I said. "Please, Wallaby."

"It's dusk."

"So what?" I said.

"I'm a crepuscular feeder."

I didn't say anything.

"You know what that means, don't you?"

"No."

"I eat at dusk. I'm hungry."

I liked the idea of dusk feeding. Somehow I knew that when I grew up, I'd feed at dusk, too. But I had to keep him going the right direction. "There's food in the forest." I got to my feet, keeping a careful eye on his paws, and smoothed the down on my chest. Then I looked back at the forest and tried to remember the names Mother had taught us. "Mossy myrtles. And eucalyptus. Lots and lots of eucalyptus."

"I eat grass. And browse on brush. They don't grow in the forest. Besides, in all those trees I can't see predators coming."

"But that means they can't see you, either," I said reasonably.

Punch.

I was back on the ground with the world spinning again.

"You don't box. Then you go and talk like a wise guy. You're no fun at all. I ought to pummel you flat." Wallaby thumped his tail in annoyance and leaned over me. "Listen up, duck. I'm going through the moor." He turned and offered his back. "Take it or leave it."

I didn't like boxing, not one bit. But I hated the idea of being alone even more. And nothing felt more right when I was worried than being on someone's back. "Onward through the moor," I said. I climbed up.

We hopped. Wallaby stopped often to forage on heath. He was a greedy fellow. If I hadn't kept urging him on, I think he might have done nothing but eat.

As evening closed in, Wallaby stopped for longer periods. The grasses here did look good, I had to admit. So I slid off his back and we ate side by side. Swallowing food dry was hard. But there was no choice; the sweet smell and sound of water didn't come from any direction.

"Don't you get thirsty?" I asked.

Wallaby struck a pose. He did that a lot. He'd hold his short arms together in front of his white chest, paws touching, curl his powerful tail around the side of his gigantic back feet, and gaze off into the distance with a wistful expression. At those times, he looked positively graceful, even to me, who knew very well what a jerky hopper and sudden boxer he was.

"You look fine," I said.

"What?"

"You look handsome. Are you trying to attract a mate?"

"What gave you that idea?"

I didn't know. Still, somehow I was sure that that was what posing was for. I'd pose someday. But, then, probably I'd be too ugly to be successful. Wallaby wasn't ugly, though. "You look great when you pose."

"Pose? Bah." Wallaby turned and struck another pose. His ear swiveled, but the rest of him stayed motionless. "I'm being vigilant. Most predators are nocturnal." He looked at me. "You do know what that means, right?"

"Not exactly."

"They hunt at night. But sometimes they're out at dusk. And that forest over there is close enough that we have to be extra vigilant."

Night predators. Fear tingled through me. Now more than ever I wanted to be in the water. I clambered up his back.

"You might as well come down again," said Wallaby. "I'll be busy eating for a while."

I slid off and came around to stand in front of him.

Wallaby regurgitated a giant plop of food.

I fluttered backward in surprise. "Well, thanks," I said hesitantly. I'd seen doves feed their young this way. And Mother had told me that the green rosella and orange-bellied parrots that were so common around Dove Lake would pump their necks and regurgitate to show their affection for another bird.

But ducks didn't do that.

Wallaby's offer lay on the ground letting off an odor that turned my stomach. "I don't mean to be an ingrate," I said, "but, well, ducks don't eat vomit."

"Did you think this was for you?" Wallaby

laughed. "You're wacky. Get your own food." He nibbled away at the mess.

I fluttered back farther. But it didn't seem polite just to stand there. So after a while, I ripped off a few blades of grass even though I'd lost my appetite.

Before long, though, I was overcome with the dryness of everything. "Don't you ever get thirsty?" I asked again.

"Not usually. I get the moisture I need from the plants I eat. But right now I do feel a little dry." He licked both paws and forearms.

I stared at him. "How can licking take away thirst?"

"What?" Wallaby laughed again. "This is how I cool down. Normally, I wouldn't travel so fast. Normally, I'd stop and enjoy breezes. But today's not normal."

"I know," I said guiltily. "Thanks. It's been kind of an awful day for me, too. My jaw aches from holding on to your fur so long. And my body's tender from flopping around when you hop. And my head hurts from where you punched me. Twice."

Wallaby thumped his tail in disgust. "Let's see

now . . . You don't box, but you do complain. No fun at all." He hopped off.

"Wait!" I ran after him. "Don't leave me. Please. I'll try to be fun."

Wallaby turned around and boxed me between the eyes again.

I looked up at him cross-eyed from the ground.

Wallaby bounced over me from one side to the other, then back. Bounce bounce, bounce. "Boxing is easy. I'll give you a lesson."

"I can't box." I stretched my wings toward him. "I don't have paws. See? Peep. I'm just a duckling. Please don't punch me again. Peep peep. I won't complain anymore. I promise. And I'll find some way to be fun. Please. Please don't leave me alone. I miss my mother. Peep. I miss my siblings. I'm not supposed to be alone."

"Hmmm." He looked at me and I was surprised to see a wave of sympathy cross his face. "I miss my mob, too."

"Mob?" I asked in alarm.

"My group. We forage together. But I got curious about some crawly animal and followed it off to that lake and look what happened. I'm off someplace I've never been before, stuck with a duck who can't even make a fist, when I belong on the same path every day with a bunch of boxing marsupials."

Marsupials? I remembered Mother explaining about them. Of course. If an animal in Tasmania had fur, it was a marsupial. "How about I ride in your pouch?"

"Are you stupid?"

"No. I'm a genius."

Wallaby grinned. His lips formed two clean white stripes in the dimming evening. "Listen, genius, only girl wallabies have pouches. I'm a boy."

"Well, I knew you were a boy, of course," I said in embarrassment. "I just didn't know only girls had pouches. Please can I stay with you? Can I ride on your back again?"

Wallaby posed. Then he let out a low sigh. "You say goofy things." His skin twitched all over, as though flies were bothering him. "That's almost fun. And we're both mobless, after all." He turned his tail to me in invitation.

I scrambled up his back to his neck. "Any chance we could make it to water by nighttime?"

"Easy. There's a pond past the forest. Lots of juicy roots grow there." His ears shot straight up and his huge back feet thumped. "Eeeeeyikes! Devil!" He bolted before I could latch on.

I went flying through the air, topsy-turvy, whap, into the tall grasses. I was about to shout to Wallaby when I smelled it. My skin tightened into little bumps everywhere. My bill clamped shut. I didn't move a muscle.

A black furry thing ran through the grass, passing so close I could see the shine of saliva in his open mouth. He was the source of that stench. I hated him. I hated his stocky legs. I hated his short, thick tail.

He made a loud, vicious screech.

I hated his voice.

And I knew immediately that he wanted to eat Wallaby. This was one of the nocturnal predators

Wallaby had been so vigilantly watching out for. "Hop, Wallaby," I said inside my head. "Hop, hop, hop. Get away safe."

I heard more screeches. Rough, but distant now. I couldn't tell if those were the screeches of pursuit or the screeches of attack. Could Wallaby's fists stand up to that monster? I shivered in fear for him. Sure, he had knocked me flat on my back three times. But he was my friend. The only friend I had. I couldn't bear to think of him at the mercy of that thing.

And, oh, what if there were more of those stinky creatures around? That one could have been a father. Maybe there was a mother. And a bunch of ravenous, stinky little babies.

I had to get out of there. I had to get to water.

I went the direction Wallaby had said the pond lay in. Traveling was tough. I tried to flutter along the tops of the grasses, but my featherless wings were close to useless. So I bushwhacked my way through them, stopping often to jump high so I could check that I was still heading the right way. Night came fast. My only guide now was the stars.

Hours passed. The grasses brushed me so dry, I felt I might wither up. The webbing between my toes chapped. Where was this pond, anyway? An easy distance for a hopping wallaby was an almost insurmountable distance for a week-old duckling. But only almost. I would surmount it—darling me. Like Mother said, if I used my head, I had a chance. I plowed on, headfirst, through the night black. Grass grass grass. On on on. Darling darling darling.

The air grew fragrant. Then the grasses changed from stiff to supple. Then the ground got soft. And wet. Positively muddy. I stumbled into the pond, giddy with gratitude.

I drank and ate and drank and ate.

This was a small pond, for sure. Leeches swam in dark inter-looping circles. Frogs croaked loudly.

But there were plenty of birds here, too. And birds were my biggest enemies. Ducks, really. So I had to be careful. I'd learned Wallaby's lesson of vigilance. I stopped often, held a pose, and watched for them. I quickly hid in the short brush whenever I sensed anyone coming my way.

The sky slowly turned rosy. Uh-oh. I'd be

easier to see in daylight. I waddled into the brush. But none of it was thick enough on this side of the pond. I needed to find a better hiding place. Fast. I yawned.

"Sleepy, huh?"

I flinched. There at the water's edge swam an animal. How had I been so unvigilant as to let it creep up on me unawares?

She climbed out onto the shore and shook off. "Time for bed."

Her words couldn't have been truer. I looked at her closely now. She was roly-poly. Shorter than Wallaby. Taller than an adult duck. For some reason her size struck me as totally perfect. And she walked on all fours, so she clearly wasn't a boxer. I took a deep whiff. Her breath smelled of grasses, roots, moss. No meat. So she wasn't a predator. And she had fur. Fur wasn't as lovely as feathers, particularly soft down. But after being on Wallaby's back for so long, I'd come to like it. A lot. And now I realized she had to have a pouch, because fur meant she was a marsupial. How lovely.

"Where's bed?" I asked as sweetly as I knew how.

"In my burrow, of course."

"Can I come?"

"You're a water bird. Sleep on the water."

"I can't. The other ducks hate me on sight. They'll kill me."

"That's odd," she said.

"It's a fact," I said sadly. "If you don't take me in, I'll have to sleep out in the open, on land." I made a pathetic sigh. When she didn't say anything, I sighed again, even more pathetically. "And one of those stinky, black, furry, horrible things will eat me."

"A Tasmanian devil, you mean? You're pretty small prey for them, don't you think? They prefer wallabies."

Poor, poor Wallaby.

"The real thing to watch out for," she said, "is quolls."

"Quolls?" I squeaked. The name chilled me.

"They have rather attractive thick snouts, I'll admit. But when they open their mouths, sharp fangs show. And they're spotted. Spots are so icky, don't you think? And they have unsightly long tails."

"I hate them," I said with fervor.

"Everyone should. Actually, they prefer eating carrion. But now and then a particularly feisty one will attack a wombat. And a coward one would even attack you." She walked into the brush, listing from side to side. Some might call that lumbering, but I thought of it as a waddle. It was terribly reassuring, especially after all this quoll talk.

I followed.

She stopped and relieved herself in front of a hole. Then she disappeared inside.

I followed.

"Go out and relieve yourself first," she said.

"Why?"

"That's what wombats do."

"I'm not a wombat."

"If you want to stay with me, you have to act like one."

I thought of that pouch of hers. That safe, cozy pouch. I scurried out of the burrow and relieved myself. Then I went back in. I walked a long way. Very long. Too long. By the time I reached her, Wombat was lying on her back with her feet in the air, already asleep. I climbed on her belly and

searched for the opening to her pouch. I planned to
wriggle down inside. But I couldn't find the opening. And I was too tired to keep searching. I settled
on the outside of the pouch, in the middle of her
tummy fur. It was as thick as Wallaby's, but much
softer. I fell instantly asleep.

CHAPTER SIX

Life as a Wombat

I WOKE in pitch black. The cool air smelled of dirt. For a second I couldn't remember where I was. Then the image of the plump wombat leading the way into her burrow came back to me. I stretched tall. "Peep," I called plaintively, feeling more babylike than ever. "Where are you, Wombat? Peep peep peep."

My voice echoed off the rocky soil. It told me I was alone. Absolutely alone. This was against rule three: Stay close. That was bad enough. But it gave me an eerie feeling that was worse than loneliness by far. Being here was wrong. My body didn't belong underground even more than it didn't belong underwater. I had to get out of here. Fast.

I stumbled around the bedchamber. Where was the tunnel? Panic rose in my chest. Ah, here was the opening. But, oh, right beside it was another tunnel opening. Which one had we come through?

And why were there two? Did some hateful predator dig its way down here while we were sleeping and drag away Wombat?

A tunnel-digging predator.

A snake.

Snakes were bad. Mother had told us. There were three types of snakes in Tasmania, and all were venomous. They were as bad as spiders.

I swallowed the peep that tried to bubble up.

Poor Wombat.

Poor me.

I followed the left tunnel, for no reason other than that I had to choose one. I waddled slowly, so that if I came across something awful—something too awful to even think—I could turn around without touching it. I stopped frequently to listen. Soon I came to another forking of tunnels. Both smelled of Wombat. Both went upward. Randomly, I chose the left again.

Vague and far-off noises reached me now. The song of a superb blue wren. The call of welcome swallows. Good noises. Merry noises. Nothing was threatening those birds. I waddled a little faster. The tunnel forked again. Without hesitation, I took the left fork. I couldn't hear the wren or the swallows anymore. But the song of a scarlet robin was unmistakable. I ran flat out.

I burst into the free, open air and tripped over a pile of wombat scat. Wombat was nowhere in sight, however. And the scat was old. A few days old at least.

It was afternoon and still very hot. I wanted to find Wombat. And I wanted to be on the water. Both wants were strong.

I had no idea where to look for Wombat. But smell and sound and wind told me the direction to go for water. I waddled quickly through grasses dotted red with poppies, holding my head high so I could stay vigilant. The farther I went, the greater my worries about Wombat grew.

"Finally woke up, huh?" Wombat basked in the sun at a burrow entrance beside a big pile of scat.

I ran to her in happy relief. "Wombat, you're alive."

"I should hope so."

I nestled against her.

"Don't get too cozy, birdy. I'm a solitary soul."

"But everyone needs friends."

"Friends?" Wombat made a little snuffle noise. "What good are friends?"

I thought back to Mother's words. "They help."

"Can you dig tunnels?"

I tried pawing the ground. I was awful at it. "You already have a tunnel," I said sensibly. "You have lots of tunnels, in fact."

"Every burrow has multiple ways in and out. Quick entry and exit are essential. You should see how many tunnels my new burrow has. It's above the creek that feeds this pond from the west, the one with so many crayfish."

"You have two burrows? Wow."

"Are you stupid?"

Was that a common marsupial question? "No, I'm a genius."

"A genius should know wombats have lots of burrows. I've got a dozen."

I put my head under my right wing to hold in another wow.

"Well," said Wombat, "if you can't dig tunnels, you can't scratch trees, either."

Trees? Trees sounded far better than burrows as a place to sleep. "Do you have tree nests, too?"

"If you're a genius, I'm a thylacine." Wombat rolled over in the dry dirt, getting her coat all dusty.

"What's a thylacine?"

"A Tasmanian tiger. They're extinct, or just about. Every now and then we wombats come across their bones as we dig a tunnel." Wombat stood up and shook off the dirt. "That means there aren't any thylacines around here. And that means I'm not one." She settled down again and closed her eyes. "Tree nests. Ha, some genius. I sleep only in burrows underground. Deep underground. I scratch trees to mark my territory."

"Oh." I poked her with my bill. "Are you going back to sleep?"

"Yup."

"But wouldn't you like a nice swim right now?"

"Nope."

"I would."

"Then go."

"Not without you." I poked her again. "You're my friend," I said hopefully.

"Then you'll have to sleep till dusk." Wombat rolled onto her back. "Like I said, if you want to stay with me, act like a wombat. A wombat sleeps in the afternoon."

"I'm not tired."

"Eat poppies. They'll knock you out."

Poppies were red. I preferred green food. Like Mother's rule: Eat greens. Oh, well. It was fairly late in the day. I supposed I could wait till dusk to swim. I climbed up on Wombat's belly and scratched around.

She opened her eyes. "What are you doing?"

"Looking for a way into your pouch."

"Birdy, you're so far from a genius it's laughable." Wombat closed her eyes again. "My pouch faces backward, so no dirt gets in it when I'm tunneling."

I approached from the right direction and wriggled into Wombat's pouch. It was a tight fit. Oh, no. I was stuck with my bill going inward instead of out toward the air. I backpedaled furiously and managed to pull myself out with a grateful peep. Then I wiggled in again, bottom first this time. With great effort, I turned onto my back, so that Wombat's pouch came up right under my bill. I felt well-tucked in. I liked this. I liked this a lot. Between the tightness and the warmth of the sun, drowsiness soon overtook me.

Water wooshed in through the nose holes in my bill. My feet started to paddle instinctively. But they were stopped short. They could barely move.

Now I was fully awake. And I remembered where I was—in Wombat's pouch. But what was all this water?

I struggled and struggled and finally pulled free. I swam up to the surface. Wombat thrashed along mindlessly in front of me.

"Hey." I glided up to her. "What's the big idea? I was sound asleep."

"And you slept good, too. Just like a wombat. So now we're swimming. You said you wanted to go swimming."

"But I was in your pouch. I could have drowned."

"You didn't." Wombat swam on.

A family of gray teals fed in the water in front of her. When they saw Wombat, they rushed away. This was good news. I hurried after Wombat. "Could you slow down a little so I can feed?"

"Wombats swim fast. And we don't stay in the water long."

This was bad news. I scarfed up underwater grasses as fast as I could.

When Wombat waddled out of the water, I waddled reluctantly behind her.

"Time for territory marking," said Wombat. "Come on, birdy, my friend. Help."

"But you already know I can't scratch trees."

"You can do what we're going to do. Anyone can." Wombat led me up a rocky ledge. She made a pile of droppings. Then she looked at me expectantly.

I looked back at her.

She made another pile of droppings and stared at me.

Oh. I got it. I made a pile of droppings.

"You learn fast." Wombat gave an approving hum.

We walked along eating brush, stopping in high places to leave scat as markings. Whenever a log or a rock was in our way, Wombat pushed it aside with her nose. She was a powerful pusher.

We passed the whole night this way. It wasn't much fun. Dawn finally broke.

"You did good, friend," said Wombat with satisfaction. "You'll make a fine wombat yet."

I didn't answer. After all, how much pride could you take in dropping scat everywhere?

"Okay, home to bed. Shall we try one of my burrows that goes under a tree? The roots offer nice nibbling."

I remembered how I'd woken up in the dark alone last time. Burrows were the pits. I shuddered. "Do you ever go north?"

"You mean like travel?"

"Yes. I'm heading north."

"Not with me, you're not. I stick to my territory." Wombat jerked her nose up sharply. "Run," she said.

She took off faster than I'd have ever thought those stumpy legs could go. But it was okay. I'd learned from my experience with Wallaby: When a marsupial makes an unexpected quick motion of any sort, latch on. So as soon as her nose went up, I had clamped my bill onto the closest bit of fur I could reach—the clump right under her neck. My body bumped against her chest as she ran. My feet dragged on the ground. I couldn't see what was chasing us, but I could hear the slipper quiet of its paws, the almost imperceptible hiss of its breath.

Wombat screamed and stopped short so fast, I went tumbling forward, down a tunnel. Phew, we were in one of Wombat's burrows.

But I was wrong. We weren't in the burrow; only I was. Wombat didn't follow. Growls and hisses and yowls and yips came from right outside the burrow entrance. I wanted to clamber up somebody's back and be safe. Wombat's back. But Wombat was out there. In a fight. Far from safe.

I waddled in a circle, holding back the frightened peeps that kept trying to burst from my bill. My friend was in trouble. I was supposed to help. That's what friends did. But I was just a duckling. I had no chance against whatever was out there.

Unless I used my head, like Mother said.

I peeked out the burrow entrance. Wombat's gray body and a strange reddish-brown body were

locked together in combat. They rolled past me and
I saw spots.

Spots! The dreaded quoll.

A long tail flopped in my face. I bit it as hard as
I could. If that wasn't using my head, nothing was.

The quoll quickly turned and looked at me with
a surprised yowl. Then his rounded ears flicked and
his eyes glared. All my courage disappeared. I cow-
ered.

In that instant, Wombat got to her feet,
knocked me back down the tunnel with her snout,
and rushed in herself. But she stopped, right there
in the entrance, with her rump facing out.

"Run," I screamed. "Run, run."

Wombat didn't budge. "Just a few minutes,"
she said.

A few minutes? For what? I waddled up to her.
The smell of blood made my down feathers stiffen to
the very calamus. The quoll growled on the other side
of Wombat. There was something off about all this.
From deep inside me came a rule no one had ever told
me: Fight or flight. Wombat wasn't doing either.

Maybe Wombat had lost her mind.

But mind or no mind, I was her friend. I wouldn't

desert her. I turned in a circle several times. Then I sat on my feet and waited.

"Okay," Wombat said at last. "He left. Let's go sleep." She waddled toward me.

I clambered onto Wombat's back in a flash. Even though the tunnel got a little bigger after the entrance, there was hardly enough room for us to pass with me on her back. But after what we'd been through, I had to be up there—I simply had to. And because she walked with her spine horizontal, it

was easy not to fall off, even if I didn't hold on with my bill. So I could talk. "Did you lose your mind?"

"Nope," said Wombat. "Did you?"

"Don't ask me that," I said. "You're the one who went bonkers."

"You bit the quoll's tail," said Wombat. "That's bonkers. Fighting back is one thing, but I've never seen anybody attack a quoll."

"You stood with your bottom to it. I've never seen anybody turn his bottom to a quoll."

"But this is your first time seeing a quoll, right?"

She had me there.

"Ha. Anyway, my rump's nothing but a big cartilage plate. If he had tried to bite it, I'd have crushed his head against the tunnel wall. He knew that. He's been around all right."

"Are you hurt bad?"

"Eh," said Wombat with a shrug that rippled under me. "It's over." She made a sucking noise.

"What are you sucking on?"

"My tooth. It broke in the fight. Maybe on a quoll bone."

I imagined breaking my own bill. That would be the end of me for sure. Poor poor Wombat. "Are you going to die in your bed?"

"Die because I broke a tooth? Are you nuts? My

83

tooth will grow out again. Wombat teeth grow continuously. You know, you say the strangest things, birdy. But that's okay. I like you."

I huddled down tighter in her fur. "I like you, too."

"It feels good having you on my back. And even better when you're in my pouch. You're almost as good as a baby wombat."

"Have you ever had a baby?" I asked.

"No. But I will. Next breeding season. I'm getting old enough."

"Good for you."

"You bet. Wombat life is good."

"Except when quolls attack."

"We're alive, aren't we? Forget about it. We'll get a good day's sleep and everything will be okay."

I was tired, in fact. But the deeper we went into this burrow, the creepier I felt. By the time we reached the bottom, I was quivering.

Wombat rolled onto her back, and I jumped off and out of the way just in time. "Talk to you later, birdy friend . . . birdy baby."

I pecked at the caked blood on her fur, slowly cleaning her all over. Those scratches must have hurt a lot. And now that I thought about it, my own feet were sore from being dragged on the ground. Wombat might think this life was good, but I thought it was tough.

I went to wriggle in her pouch, then remembered waking underwater. Nope, it was better to sleep on top of her tummy. So long as she didn't leave me here.

"Take me with you when you wake up," I said. "I don't like to be left in the burrow all alone."

But she was already asleep.

CHAPTER SEVEN

Geese

I WOKE alone again. In pitch black. I knew it. I just knew this would happen. Burrows were lousy places. I vowed never to go this deep again. If I ever made it out of here, that is.

That was a bad way to think. I had to remain calm. There were lots of ways out. And Wombat was undoubtedly resting at the end of one of them. I'd find her. Soon.

But the air was too earthy. The walls of the

bedchamber were too close. Everything was too dark. Panic seized me. I ran like a maniac up the first tunnel I found, taking the left branch of every fork. Whatever possessed Wombat to dig these tunnels so long?

I ran and ran and plunged into something that covered my head, my chest, my back. It was thin, like skin. It made it hard to breathe. I was going to suffocate. Something crawled from my head down my back, between my wings. Something with lots of legs. A spider! I had run straight into a spider-web. I was a dead duckling. I peeped and the silky mess got in my mouth.

I ran and burst into the afternoon sunshine, breathless, and kept running until I sloshed into a fresh pile of Wombat scat. "Wombat," I called. "Where are you?"

"Maybe we should change your name from Genius to Idiot." Wombat waddled up behind me. "A water bird out on land should know better than to make a lot of noise. It's like you're saying, 'Here I am, quoll. Dinner.'"

"I'm going to die!" I screamed. "A spider got me. Good-bye, dear Wombat."

"Roll," said Wombat.

"What?"

"Lie down and roll."

I rolled and rolled.

"Stop already," said Wombat after a long while.

I stood up and let out a relieved peep. "I'm still alive."

"Of course you are. Look at those egg sacs."

I looked at the lumpy egg sacs clumped through the wads of silk on the ground around me.

"That shape, bigger at one end, that tells you these are from a cave spider. They're hardly a bother. It's the funnel web and redbacks you have to watch out for. But, since you're not the brightest fellow, you're better off just to avoid all webs."

What a fool I was. I knew so little about anything. But at this moment I knew one thing really well. "Wombat, I have something to tell you."

"I'm listening."

"I'm sad to say it, Wombat, but I don't like this burrow."

"Don't be silly. The cave spider picked a tunnel

I haven't used for a long time. But I can go through all the tunnels, clearing them out for you. You won't run into any more webs."

"It's not just spiders," I said. "I don't like this burrow."

"I'm a great tunnel digger. What's wrong with it?"

"Nothing, as far as burrows go. I just hate all burrows."

"What?" Wombat looked shocked. "Wombats live in burrows. That's what we do. You can't be a wombat if you won't live in a burrow."

And there was the wrenching truth. "I'm sorry, Wombat, but I think the life of a wombat isn't for me."

Wombat didn't say anything. She just made a quiet snort. After a while, she lay down on her side. "Oh, well." She snorted again and rolled so her back was to me. "There's no sense in crying. A wombat needs to be sensible."

I listened to her snuffling and I choked up. But I couldn't face going down into a burrow again. "Maybe we could build a nest together some-place."

"Don't be silly. I'm a wombat. You're a water bird. That's how it is." Wombat got to her feet. "Go out on the water."

"I don't want to go without you."

"You'll be safe. Quolls don't swim."

"I'll miss you. Besides, the other ducks will kill me. I told you. They hate me on sight."

"Ducks? Only ducks? Not the other water birds?"

"Only ducks," I said.

"Well then, problem solved," said Wombat. "I know where there are other water birds that aren't ducks. I'll take you to them."

I thought about that. "I could never live with egrets," I said at last. "They don't even swim. And grebes would be pretty tough. They dive way down deep, and I hate diving. And swamphens, well, they're afraid of me."

"Don't feel bad. Swamphens are afraid of everyone. Anyway, the birds I know of are geese."

Geese? There were no geese at Dove Lake. But I knew some things about geese anyway. They rolled their eggs. The freckled duck had told Mother that. I heard it from inside my shell. And once Mother had told Father that she'd get a new mate next year—she wasn't a goose. So geese must keep their mates.

These were okay facts. Rolling eggs, well, that was odd, but it couldn't be bad, really. And I positively liked the idea that geese kept the same mates year after year. It felt right. "Geese might be nice birds," I said. "Okay, I'll give it a try. Please introduce me to your geese friends."

"They're not my friends. You helped mark my territory. You bit the quoll's tail. You rode on my back and nestled in my pouch. You're my friend. But these geese guys, I've never even talked with them. I don't vouch for them. I just know where they hang out. So I'll bring you there. But then you're on your own. Think you can handle it?"

I suppressed a babyish peep. This wasn't the moment to remind Wombat how young I was. "Let's go."

"I'd prefer waiting till dusk," said Wombat. She looked me up and down. I waddled in place anxiously.

"But it's kind of far," said Wombat. "So if we waited, they might be gone."

I waddled and waddled. I shook my tail encouragingly.

"Soooo," said Wombat, "follow me."

"Yippee!" I said.

"Not so loud," said Wombat. "It's always best not to call attention to yourself."

Wombat ran along rocks. I hopped behind her. Then she plowed through high grasses, crushing them in a nice trail that I waddled through easily. Fairly often, she stopped to browse. But that was okay; I was hungry, too.

The sun faded.

"Are we close?" I asked.

"Not too far," said Wombat.

We'd be among these strangers soon. The thought made me feel itchy all over. "What do you know about geese?" I asked. "Besides where they are, I mean."

"Not much."

"What do they look like?"

"Ducks. Only bigger. And their necks are longer."

Long necks sounded good. But the bigness kind of worried me. Teals had almost managed to drown me. If geese were bigger, they were stronger. If they tried to kill me, they'd succeed.

On the other hand, I never wanted to go down a wombat burrow again, no matter how much I cared about Wombat. And I didn't want to be alone. "I'm not afraid," I said to Wombat.

We walked and walked.

"How much farther?" I asked.

"Not much."

"I'm not afraid," I said.

We walked and walked.

"Are we there yet?" I said.

"Almost."

"I'm not afraid," I said.

We walked. Then Wombat stopped. "We're here."

"I'm afraid," I said. "Burrows aren't so bad really. Let's go back."

"Don't you want to take a look first?"

That didn't seem too dangerous. I climbed onto Wombat's back and looked out over the high grass. In a pasture just beyond the grass's edge two big birds waddled together. They were pale gray with black on the end of their tails. Circles of black that looked sort of like eyes speckled the tips of their wings. They had pink legs, black feet, and short black bills. At the top of their bills a bright yellow-green band of flesh crossed the nostrils. A cere. Mother had told us that the dreaded goshawk had a yellow cere. These geese didn't match anything else she said about goshawks, though. And these fellows' ceres were more green than yellow, really. They were busily feeding on tussock and spear grass and clover. Nothing about them was particularly pleasant, so far as I could see. They were nowhere near as fine to look at as Mother. And their necks weren't, in fact, very long at all. But nothing about them was terribly scary, either.

If only they wouldn't kill me.

"Well?" said Wombat. "It's them or me."

Wombat, for all her wonderful qualities, was a burrow creature. Geese were water birds. Despite the loss of Wombat and the wretchedness of the risk these new creatures posed, I didn't really have a choice. "You've been a fine friend," I said softly. "As fine as anyone could ask."

"Go already," said Wombat.

I jumped to the ground.

Wombat turned and trotted away.

"Thanks," I called after her. But quietly. Maybe too quietly for her to hear. She didn't look back. I could see the very tip of her short tail as she waddled away. It struck me as endearing. She'd be a terrific mother. "Bye," I called even more softly. "Bye-bye."

I turned to face the geese. One big deep breath. I could do this. I waddled slowly across the pasture.

A goose looked at me.

I stopped.

He went back to feeding.

I waddled closer to them.

The same goose looked at me.

I stopped.

He went back to feeding.

I waddled closer.

Now both of them looked at me.

I stopped.

They kept looking at me this time. Their bills were the color of the stones Wombat and I had dropped scat on the night before, and I bet they were just as hard.

What was I doing here? I could be riding on Wombat's wide back.

But it was too late now. Another big deep breath. I waddled closer still.

"Honk," said one of them.

"Grunt," said the other.

"Who are you?" they chorused.

"Ugly." It was my name, after all.

"I'll say," said one of them. "Honk, honk."

"Ugly ugly ugly," said the other. "Grunt, grunt, grunt."

They strutted in a circle around me.

"We're important," said Honker. "We're ganders. Young, strong ganders."

"We know our stuff," said Grunter.

I stood rock still and tried to look like I knew my stuff, too.

Honker finally stopped in front of me. "You're so ugly, I like you."

"Me, too," said Grunter. "You're kind of cool. You can hang with us and we'll show you off."

"Peep," I said in relief.

"Peep? Are you kidding? Peep? Is that the only call you can make?" said Grunter.

"Pretty much," I said.

"Listen to us," said Grunter. "Bark bark bark!" He butted Honker in the side of the neck.

"Bark bark bark!" said Honker, obligingly.

"That's a sea-lion bark," said Grunter. "Did it scare you?"

"Yes."

Grunter wagged his tail proudly and ripped off a thatch of grass. He swallowed, then barked, then ate some more.

"Eat," said Honker.

I looked at the grasses and thought about how hard it was to swallow them dry. "On the whole," I said hopefully, "I'd rather eat in the water."

"Weird," said Grunter. "Ungooselike. We sleep in the water sometimes, but we eat on land."

"Or in swamps," said Honker. "Can you fly, Ugly?"

"I don't think so."

"Stretch your wings," said Honker.

I stood tall and stretched my wings.

"No flight feathers yet," said Grunter. "Grunt, grunt, grunt. That means we can't take you to the off shore islands. Too bad. You could have heard the sea lions and seen for yourself how really great we are at mimicking their bark." He stretched tall and ruffled his feathers, and for a minute I thought he was going to bark again. But then he settled down and said, "The Furneaux Islands are the best. All the Cape Barren geese go there. That's what we are: Cape Barren geese. Grunt grunt grunt."

"We can go to the swamp near Cape Portland, though," said Honker. "It's not too far to walk. And there are bound to be geese there. Probably plenty of eligible young females." He strutted back and forth. Then he stopped and looked at me. "Where were you hatched?"

"Dove Lake."

"Never been there," said Honker, "but I've heard about it. It's near the tallest mountain in Tasmania. And the water's sweet. You like salty water, too though, not just sweet water, right?"

"Right," I said without hesitation. Somehow I knew I could drink any water.

"Good," said Grunter. "The cape swamp is brackish."

"Okay," said Honker. "Let's hit the road. Honk, honk. I can't wait to be back with a flock." He leaned toward me. "We Cape Barren geese are gregarious, you know."

"I'm gregarious, too," I said happily. Mother had told me.

"Yeah?" said Grunter. "Good. We got driven out by a grumpy old gander. But we'll find a flock to take us all in. Oh, I'm feeling good about this, I really am. And we can eat as we go. Honker, remember that field of hops? It's on the way."

"I remember the farmer yelling at us." Honker shook his chest. "And those awful, baying dogs."

"Don't be such a scaredy swamphen," said Grunter. "Farmers and dogs can't fly. We got away last time. We'll get away this time. And the food's so good."

What about me? Whatever a farmer or a dog was, they'd come after me, too, and I couldn't fly. How would I get away?

But Honker and Grunter were already waddling fast through the wildflowers. I waddled after them. We went at a pretty good clip, stopping only to eat the occasional succulent and honk (or in my case, peep) at the occasional lizard.

It was a long time before we reached the tall hops. Honker and Grunter ate and ate. This had been a hard day for me so far. Eating dry food scratched my throat. Still, the rich taste of hops was an experience worth having. And they gave me a wondrously full feeling.

"Aren't you glad we came this way?" said Grunter.

"Honk," said Honker.

"Peep," I chimed in. These were pretty good guys. I couldn't believe my luck. Mother had said all anyone really needed was one good friend, and here I was with two. They lacked the warmth of Wombat. But they had a certain charm of their own.

Satiated and happy, we left the field behind and waddled, waddled, waddled over the moor till the land grew wet and the air smelled salty and sour.

Grunter stopped. "I wonder if we should practice first."

"Practice?" said Honker.

"Yeah. We've never done it before."

"Okay," said Honker. "Good idea. Ugly can be the female."

"What?" I chirped. "I'm a boy."

"We know that. Grunt grunt. It's just pretend. So we can practice."

"Practice what?" I asked worriedly.

By this time Honker had walked away several steps. "Honk!" He came waddling back at me with his head low in front and his neck rippling oddly.

I stepped back to get out of the way. "Are you sick?"

Honker stood tall and waddled in a circle. "Did I look sick? Oh no. Hey, Grunter, did you think I looked sick?"

"You looked great," said Grunter. "Ugly doesn't know squat. My turn." He gave a grunt and came at me the same way Honker did.

This time I tried to stand my ground. But at the last moment I lost heart and backed away again.

"What'd you think?" said Grunter.

"Great," said Honker. "Just like you said. We're both great. We're both terrific. We're the best ganders ever." He looked at me. "Your turn."

I stuck my head forward and waddled toward Honker.

"No no no," said Grunter. "Your neck's all wrong."

"Undulate it, like this." Honker lowered his head and walked forward with his neck rippling like water in the wind.

I tried. Not much happened.

"Awful," said Grunter. "Females won't notice that at all. Can you fight?"

I remembered Wallaby. "Ducks don't box," I said quickly.

"Ducks? Box? What are you talking about?" Grunter swung his head from side to side. "Don't

go talking all nutso on me now, Ugly. Pay attention. If two ganders want the same female, they fight for her."

"I don't want a female goose," I said. "I'm a baby. Peep."

"Well, we do," said Grunter. "So if we get in a fight with strangers, pitch in on our side."

"Sure," I said. "I fought a quoll."

"What?" said Grunter.

"Don't lie," said Honker.

"It's true," I said. "When I lived with Wombat."

"You lived with a wombat?" Grunter sidled up

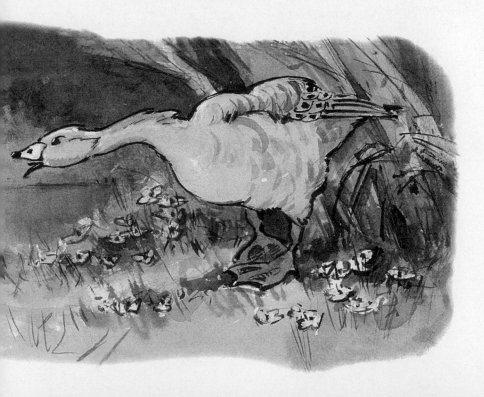

to Honker. He looked over his shoulder at me. Then he put his bill to Honker's earhole.

I strained to hear.

"He's off his rocker," said Grunter.

"No I'm not," I piped up.

"Remember the big fight at the start of last breeding season?" said Honker.

"You mean the one between the grumpy old gander and the young one?" said Grunter. "Who could forget? Grunt grunt grunt."

"The young one died. And he was really strong. Honk honk." Honker came over to me. "You're small, Ugly," he said quietly. "Maybe you fought a quoll and maybe you didn't. But no matter what, forget what Grunter said. If we get in a fight, you stay clear."

I didn't answer. These were my friends. If they needed my help, I'd give it.

We glided into the shallow water. Ah, swamp was so good. I ate underwater grass. And lots of pink bladderwort. Bliss. This was pure bliss.

Honker swam close. "Don't say anything," he murmured so softly I could hardly hear. "Sorry to say it, but you're kind of stupid and that will ruin things."

"Yeah, let us do the talking," said Grunter. "Go hide."

Talking to who? I didn't see anyone else. But I held back among the reeds obligingly anyway.

"Where are the other geese?" said Honker loudly. "Honk honk honk. Where are you?" He swam out into the open.

"Grunt grunt grunt grunt," said Grunter. "Come look at us. We're here. Come on girly-geese. You want us. We're the best. If you hurry, it's not too late to have a whole slew of goslings this season. Come on. Grunt grunt grunt."

Bang!

A flock of geese erupted from the reeds.

Bang! Bang!

Honker collapsed.

Grunter collapsed.

The water near them turned blood red. I swam frantically to my downed friends. They weren't moving.

Bang, bang, bang came from the moor. *Bang, bang, bang* came from the trees.

Geese fell in terrifying spirals, plopping into

the swamp. Acrid smoke lingered in the wet air. Everything was chaos.

Splash, splash! A tall, four-legged, hairy creature bounded past. It was brown with long, floppy ears and a straight tail. Another followed. The second one stopped and looked at me. His huge tongue lolled out of his mouth. He pushed his nose into my chest. It was black and flat, just like Wombat's nose. But this creature was nothing like my good friend Wombat. He lifted his top lip to reveal pointed teeth. His breath smelled of blood and bones. I was doomed. "What are you?" he said in a rolling growl.

I couldn't answer. I couldn't even scream. I could hear Mother telling me to use my head, but I felt like I didn't have a head.

"Scrawny, scraggly thing." He twirled away, picked up the body of Honker in his mouth, and bounded back the way he'd come.

I swam into the reeds and stopped there, petrified.

The bangs and splashes went on for a long time. I stayed put through it all. When it finally stopped, the air rang. The clouds stank.

I still stayed put.

CHAPTER EIGHT

A Haven

THE UNNATURAL silence that followed all that violence slowly yielded as night came. Insects chirruped in the reeds. Birds fluttered in the trees. A fish jumped with a small splish.

Thoughts gradually crept back into my brain. Honker and Grunter were dead. Lots of other geese had died here, too. This swamp was a bad place.

A snake zigzagged past with his head held

high out of the water. His eyes gleamed in the moonlight.

Then a white-breasted sea eagle flew over the swamp. I'd never seen sea birds before, but I recognized this one from the days when Mother was busily describing the whole world to us ducklings. Sea birds didn't belong so far inland. Every part of me said this went against nature. A bad omen.

A jagged line of light split the sky. *Boom!*

No doubt about it: Time to get out of here.

I swam from the reeds to the shore. I had no plan but to put as much distance as I could between myself and that swamp before I gave way to exhaustion. I would go fast. But I would be vigilant—a lesson from Wallaby—and quiet—a lesson from Wombat and, inadvertently and sadly, from Honker and Grunter.

Within minutes, however, speed became an unreachable dream. I was bogged down by rain. Not just the ordinary rain I'd experienced back at Dove Lake. That rain brought a welcome respite from the heat. No, this was torrential. Fat drops hammered my head and back. They came so thick, they blocked out the moon. I couldn't see a thing.

And I suddenly I understood what the sea eagle was doing here. He'd been blown off course by the storm. I thought of his big wings stretching out from that muscular chest. He was strong. That meant this storm was dangerous.

Against all my instincts, I actually longed for a wombat tunnel. I lifted my chin to sniff for wombat droppings. Rain clogged my nose holes.

I waddled blindly with my neck curled downward. Honker and Grunter were dead. And their death had come without warning. Those important ganders. Young and strong. Ganders who knew their stuff. Though I was but a duckling, I sensed the immensity of all they had missed out on. And I knew I didn't want to miss out on those things. I wanted my flight feathers to come in. When winter arrived in Tasmania, I wanted to migrate north to the milder mainland. And in a couple of years I wanted to find a mate and have a clutch. And then another clutch the next year. And another the year after that. I wanted lots of clutches. Ugly as I was, I wanted life.

Something ran across the path behind me. Whatever it was, it didn't stop. A wallaby passed on my right side. The rain made everything so dark, I wouldn't have even known what he was, but for the hopping sound that was so familiar to me. He didn't stop, either. I kept waddling.

Winds rose from every direction. They swirled, pushing me hither and thither. They howled. They tore branches from beech trees and pine trees and tossed them randomly. Wild winds. But I kept waddling—away, away, away from the swamp of death.

And there, in front of me, was a light. It wasn't the sun, of course. But it wasn't the moon, either. Or even a star. It didn't twinkle. It glowed. I waddled toward it, swept along by that meddling wind, much faster than my cautious heart wanted to go.

Now I could make out some sort of wooden dwelling. The light was inside it. I could see it through a big hole in the wood.

I waddled closer, until I was standing beneath the hole. I screwed up my courage and jumped. *Smack*. My bill had hit something that sent me falling, *splat* on my back. A transparent sheet covered the hole. Transparent and hard. It hurt. And I hadn't even gotten a good look inside.

Clank.

Part of the dwelling flopped open-and-closed, open-and-closed. A loose board tossed by the wind. *Clank. Clank.*

The rain seemed to pick up, if that was possible. The wind grew more fierce. It pressed me against the side of this home. It soaked me to the core. I shivered. What was I thinking? Even a sea eagle had sought shelter from this storm. The wind and rain would surely kill me if I didn't get somewhere safe fast.

Clank, went the loose board. *Clank. Clank.*

Each time it opened, I got a glimpse of the interior of the dwelling. Lit and dry. I didn't see anyone inside, but a place that nice couldn't be empty. And the creatures living there might be hideous. They might run on four legs and have long straight tails and bad breath. They might eat geese. And other things.

Clank. Clank.

The board flopped open just wide enough for a body about my size to squeeze through, if it was fast enough. But if it was too slow, the board would smack it. And with this wind, the board might even crush it.

I waddled toward the loose board.

Clank. Clank.

I stood directly by it now, every part of me alert.

It opened and I zipped in before I could give it another thought. *Slap*, came the noise behind me as the board hit my backside. Ouch.

The place reeked with unfamiliar and frightening smells. I waddled quickly across a layer of pine needles to a corner beneath a high piece of wood, settled my body onto my feet, tucked my head under my right wing, and sought refuge in sleep.

"Purrrrrr."

My eyes shot open.

Two green predator eyes stared at me so close, I could feel the animal's body heat. It crouched in front of me. Its long tail curled around its side and the tip of it twitched.

Death stared me in the face.

I shut my eyes again.

"Wake up," he said. "I'm a tomcat. What are you?"

A cat. I knew nothing about cats. But this one's

breath smelled of fish and other things too disgusting to figure out. I didn't move.

"What's your name?"

I didn't want to say my name anymore. After what happened to Honker and Grunter, it felt like bad luck.

"Come on. Don't be boring."

I opened one eye.

"It's not a chicken," came a scratchy voice. "Pa-kok."

I opened the other eye.

"Pa-kok," said the second creature. "Pa-kok, pa-kok, pa-kok. I'm a chicken. I should know." She was a bird, white with brown speckles and a brown head. She had a sharp, small, downward curved beak and yellow scaly feet. Her legs were short, but her toes were long and they ended in thick black claws. This was no water bird, that was for sure. "Pa-kok."

"What's going on down there?" A third creature, a gigantic one, peered under at us. The parts of her that I could see were skinny. But her head was round and she sprouted long black wavy strings from the top of it, with strands of gray mixed in.

Most of her was covered with some odd blue stuff. Her appearance was altogether comical. "What have you found, Mapali Cat and Pama Chick?" She got onto her knees and leaned forward, squinting. "What's this? A bird? I hope it's a mutton bird. I love mutton birds." She put her hand out and felt around. I shrank back, but she managed to touch my face. "I can make out a beak. No, a bill. Oh, my, is it a duck? Pama Chick, tell me. Is it really a duck?"

"I hate it when Old Woman asks me questions," said Pama Chick. "She never understands my answers, so what's the point? Pa-kok."

"You just don't know the answer," said Mapali Cat. "If you knew what this creature was, you'd tell Old Woman even if she can't understand." He pushed his head against the arm of Old Woman. "Purrrrrrr."

"You don't know what it is, either," said Pama Chick.

"Ah, duck," said Old Woman, absentmindedly giving Mapali Cat a scratch behind the ear. "When I was little, we used to find duck eggs on the *katina*—the beach. What a treat." She came fully under the table and sat with her long, thin legs crossed in front of her. Mapali Cat jumped onto her lap. She petted his whole head now. The cat arched his back and purred.

I liked Old Woman. Anyone who enjoyed the beauty of a duck egg had to be good. I studied the mop of strings on her head. Why, that was fur. Scraggly fur, but fur, sure enough. She was a marsupial. Maybe I could climb into her pouch. If only that meat-eating cat would move aside, I'd give it a try.

"We can feed this duck," said Old Woman cheerfully. "And as soon as it feels safe and happy, it will lay us eggs. Your eggs are good, Pama Chick, but duck eggs will be a fine addition. Oooo, I hope it's not a drake."

"It's a boy, it's a boy, it's a boy," said Pama Chick. "How dumb can human beings be? The human family that lived in this house before Old Woman was just as stupid. Any bird knows this thing is a boy."

"I knew it was a boy," said Mapali Cat. "So it's not just birds that can tell. You don't know anything I don't know."

"You can't lay eggs," said Pama Chick.

"You can't arch your back," said Mapali Cat.

"You can't cluck," said Pama Chick.

"You can't purr," said Mapali Cat.

"You can't fly," said Pama Chick.

"You call what you do flying? I can get higher in trees than you can."

Pama Chick pecked Mapali Cat.

Mapali Cat hissed and spat.

"Yes," said Old Woman. She pushed the cat off her lap and pressed her hands together. "Let's welcome this duck into our *lenna*—our home."

Human beings might be too stupid to tell males from females, but Old Woman was certainly a fine creature anyway. I prepared to leap for her pouch.

"We'll feed her," said Old Woman. "Fatten her up good." She crawled out from under the table and walked away chanting. She fingered her shell necklace and swayed rhythmically.

Mapali Cat and Pama Chick followed her, the cat yowling and the chick pa-koking.

They formed a little line. It was almost like a mother duck with two ducklings. They were having fun.

It had been a long time since I'd had any fun.

They wound through the room, chanting, yowling, pa-koking.

It was just too wonderful. I joined the line, peeping sonorously.

Every now and then, the blue stuff that covered Old Woman would flutter out from her legs, and I'd make a jump for her pouch. Each time, she stumbled and shooed me aside and danced on.

After a while, Old Woman collapsed onto her bed. Mapali Cat and Pama Chick settled near her.

Finally, I could get into Old Woman's pouch. I fussed about, trying to dig my way under that blue stuff.

Old Woman swatted my head. "Just what do you think you're doing, digging at my skirt like that? You better not be any trouble. I'm willing to feed you, but only if you're good. Because I'll get eggs in return. Or, if you turn out to be a drake, I can eat you. Young duck is almost as good as young mutton bird. But you have to be good. Hear that?"

I gulped. Old Woman was more dangerous than she looked. I jumped away and backed against the wall.

For the next three weeks I ate well and life was okay. So long as Old Woman didn't figure out I was a drake, I was safe.

She put down a big bowl of fresh water every-day, and she offered me the same root mash she gave Pama Chick. It wasn't great food. But Old Woman was a bit careless by nature, and with age had lost a good deal of her sight. So she dropped a lot of things on the floor. Whenever she prepared a meal for herself, I stood at her feet. So did Pama Chick.

"Pa-kok," screamed Pama Chick. "I get the tree ferns, I get the tree ferns. They make my egg yolks have a deep orange color.

"Pa-kok," screamed Pama Chick. "I get the currants. I get the currants. They make my feathers shine.

"Pa-kok," screamed Pama Chick. "I get everything. I get everything. Just because, just because, just because."

But I was young and fast, and Pama Chick was an aging hen. So we both got plenty. And neither of us had to compete with Mapali Cat, who hunted down his own food outside at night.

I had the full run of Old Woman's home, because she scattered pine needles all over the floor to catch Pama Chick's droppings, and now mine as well. Every few days, she swept it all out and scattered fresh needles. It was a good system.

Much of the day Old Woman sat in a chair by the hole I'd learned to call a window, and stroked Mapali Cat, who purred so loud, my bill reverberated. She told stories about her childhood. Her

voice filled with a keen longing that felt familiar to
my own heart. I listened closely.

"My family was big. Now they're all gone."
Her voice was a sad singsong. "I'm alone, but for
you, Mapali Cat, and, you, Pama Chick, and you,
little duck."

I waddled over and settled on her bony feet, to
warm them.

"We spoke Palawa Kani. We lived outside
except when the weather was bad. Then we did
this." Old Woman lay on the floor and wriggled on
her belly. "We slithered through underground
tunnels, so narrow, my father hardly fit."

I remembered Wombat's tunnels, and I shivered.

"We held our heads up, above the water that
flowed slowly through those channels."

I shivered harder.

"We came out into cave rooms where we could
stand. Mother gave us a little lemon juice, to fight
off chest colds, after being in the water like that.
We lit a fire. Oh, my, it felt good to have room to
move again. So we danced." Old Woman danced in
place. "We ate and told stories until we fell
asleep."

Old Woman laughed. "We loved those cave rooms. We decorated the walls. We filled our mouths with pigment mix and sprayed it over our hands." She went to the stove and filled her mouth with the brown drink she liked so much. Then she put both hands on the wall and spit on them. When she took her hands away, the brown left behind handprint outlines. "We had lots of colors."

I imagined big and little handprints all over the rocks. It was an odd thing to do, but I liked the idea.

"It was beautiful," crooned Old Woman.

I believed her.

"In mutton bird season, we got in bark boats. It was scary. But, oh, it was exciting." She put her hand over her forehead as though she was screening out the sun. "We set out on a calm sea to Swan Island."

Swan? Whatever that meant, the very word attracted me. It had a lilt to it.

"But the sea was deceptive. The current gets fast near that island. We could land only on the far-side beach, never on the rocks, or the waves would dash us to bits." She shook her head. "And then there were the snakes."

I quivered all over.

"Swan Island is infested with them. But they make good eating."

She pretended to hold a snake in one hand and skin it with the other. Old Woman really was fierce.

"In the morning we waited for the rising tide to carry us west, across the strait. We had to be fast. If we didn't beat the ebb tide, we could get pulled backward and crash on the Moriarty Banks."

I stepped from foot to foot in worry.

"But we always made it. To Clarke Island. A windy place. You could never get out of the wind."

I tightened my wings to my sides.

"But that was good. Because the wind saved us from those tiny flies. Ugh, how they bit." She made a little spasm at the memory. "But the fish and abalone were abundant. And delicious."

I wasn't interested in eating fish. And what was abalone?

"After a couple of days we headed to Cape Barren Island."

Cape Barren Island? Honker and Grunter were Cape Barren geese. I listened extra close.

"We hunted seals there. There's no meat on earth better than that."

She sure had awful eating habits.

"Then we went to Badger Island and finally, oh, finally, to Mount Chappell Island. That's where the mutton birds were." She settled into her chair and pointed vaguely in my direction. "The taste will stay with me for the rest of my life. You'll remind me of it, if you're a drake, little duck. Oh, yes."

I dashed to the corner and hid.

"All summer long we drank seawater in the morning. That's what kept us healthy." She clapped her hands. "We were so strong in those days, we could climb the mountain to the top, the very top. From Mount Chappell we saw out in every direction. Forever." Old Woman's head drooped forward. "Forever and ever. That's where I really belong. Not here. Not in some house built by strangers." She fell asleep in her chair.

When she woke, she shuffled around the room and stroked Mapali Cat fast the wrong way till sparks flew from his fur. It was a spectacle.

Every now and then Mapali Cat stretched and gave up his position in Old Woman's lap. Then Pama Chick would flutter up there and push her head under Old Woman's hand. That hen actually liked to be petted. The more Old Woman petted her, the happier she got.

A few times Old Woman slapped her knee and invited me to come up for a petting. I never did. Those hands were dangerous. She considered me a potential meal, after all. Mother's first rule was always in the back of my mind: Don't get eaten.

Old Woman would cross her arms at her chest and peer down toward me. "We never had pets when I was a child," she said. "Animals should be free, just like people. But when I came to this house, the chicken who lays *pama* egg—one egg—a day, was already here, and the cat who gives *mapali* purrs—plenty of purrs—was already here. And now I'm used to them." She smiled in my general direction. "But you stay wild, little duck. That's fine with me. So long as you start laying eggs soon. Another couple of months."

So that's all I had to count on, another couple of months.

When Old Woman wasn't telling stories, I wandered around the rooms, exploring and reexploring every nook and cranny, trying to steer clear of Mapali Cat and Pama Chick's arguments. I acted agreeable. Peaceable. Like Mother said: Pacific black ducks are peaceable. It was an effort for me, though. I was growing irritable as my loneliness went on. I had to work very hard to keep from snapping when one of them said something nasty.

Night was even lonelier: I slept alone. That's when I missed Wombat most, with her thick fur and soft snuffles. It hurt to remember. And I wouldn't even let myself think about how my siblings and I used to sleep in a big pile, wiggling and jiggling each other comfortably all night—that was way too painful. But food and safety were worth a lot. I tried to focus on the good things of this life.

Then one day while Old Woman was out, everything changed.

"It's too hot," said Pama Chick. "I can't wait for winter."

"The best time of the year," said Mapali Cat. "Nothing's better than sitting on the wide ledge inside the window in a room toasty from the hearth fire, looking out at the snow."

"Nothing except perching on the back of the chair and looking out," said Pama Chick.

"No, the ledge by the window is better," said Mapali Cat.

"Migrating is better yet," I said.

"You talk! Pa-kok. All this time I thought you could only peep, but you actually talk."

"And you're stupid," said Mapali Cat.

"And wrong. Pa-kok, pa-kok."

"I'm not stupid or wrong," I said forcefully, my down fluffing out with feelings that surprised me. They were hardly peaceable. They were downright belligerent. My dear mother would have been dismayed.

"Can you lay eggs?" asked Pama Chick.

"You know I can't."

"Can you purr and arch your back and let off sparks?" asked Mapali Cat.

"Of course not."

"Then shut up," said Pama Chick. "And listen to what we say. We know everything."

I clacked my bill. "You don't know everything."

"What?" Mapali Cat jumped down from the table where he'd been resting. "I dare you to say that again."

"You disagree with each other a lot," I said pointedly. "So you can't both be right all the time."

"That's stupid," said Mapali Cat. He circled me slowly.

"You're stupid," said Pama Chick. She got up off her nest and circled me the other direction.

I lifted myself to my full height. My flight feathers still hadn't come in, but I was much taller than I'd been when I first came to this home. It's amazing how fast I'd grown. Mapali Cat and Pama Chick should have been impressed. Instead, they circled closer.

I spread my skinny wings and cocked them at the elbows threateningly. I lowered my head and let out a loud hiss. They still circled, closer and closer.

I jumped and landed on the seat of Old Woman's chair. From there it was an easy jump to the ledge inside the window. The sunshine streamed in. Pama Chick was right; it was hot. All at once I didn't care about the ill-tempered beasts inside this home. I could think only of the outdoors. "Wouldn't it be great to be swimming right now?" I said. "On a nice deep lake."

"Swimming?" said Mapali Cat. "What a revolting idea."

"He's lost his marbles," said Pama Chick. "You never swim. I never swim. Even Old Woman never swims, and she's got some oddball ways."

"Gliding through cool waters. Reaching my head down under to rip off yummy grasses. Ahhh." I hadn't realized till that moment how very much I missed water life. I almost swooned.

"Pay attention, Duck," said Pama Chick. "That's sick talk. Friends tell you the truth, even when it's ugly. You're sick sick sick. Act like us and you'll get better. Pa-kok."

The word *ugly* snapped me out of my reverie. I knew about ugly, all right. It was my ugliness that had caused me so much trouble. And Pama Chick's words were the ugly thing.

I knew about friends, too. Wallaby and Wombat and Honker and Grunter. They were friends. Mapali Cat and Pama Chick didn't know the first thing about friendship. And they didn't know the first thing about how I should live my life. I was a wild water bird.

I didn't want to wind up like Old Woman, escaping into dreams to be where I really belonged. The life I was meant for was out there. Waiting.

"I'm leaving," I said.

"Just how do you think you'll get out?" said Pama Chick.

"The door and window are closed," said Mapali Cat.

"I'll break the window," I said.

"With what?" said Pama Chick. "Even your block of a head isn't that hard."

"And you'll get cut," said Mapali Cat.

"Well, I'm going to get out." Now that I'd said it, the desire to do it overwhelmed me. My neck, my wings, my feet, all of me tensed with need. "Somehow. I'm leaving. For good."

"For good?" Mapali Cat licked his paw. "Well, good riddance."

"You'll be sorry," said Pama Chick. "But we won't."

I hopped down to the floor and waited by the door.

When Old Woman came home, I rushed past her.

"Stop," she screamed, running after me.

But she was old. And I was young.

And the outdoors was my world.

CHAPTER NINE

Cold

IT AMAZED me the loneliness that a young duck could get used to. I lived on a pond now, sur-rounded by mountains, totally alone. Oh, there were lots of other water birds here. Many kinds of ducks, as well as grebes and swamphens. There was even a small group of geese on an island near the middle of the pond. But they ignored me, every one of them. I had grown so large that ducks were afraid to taunt me these days. I was bigger than all of them. I was bigger than the geese, too. Sometimes I wondered if I'd ever stop growing.

There were advantages to size: brown falcons flew overhead and I didn't bother to hide. Not much scared me.

Except the thought of being alone forever.

All I needed, all anyone needed, was one good friend. When Mother had said that, it seemed easy. Now it seemed so hard.

But I had to admit I was lucky to find this place. A lot of the world is dry and empty. It took many days of wandering before I happened upon my new pond home. The water was vivid blue and tasty grasses grew up from the bottom silt. I could bear this life.

I passed my days and nights gliding and sleeping. I fed mostly at dusk. I took up an interest in cloud formations. I watched the sky and I learned to predict the weather.

Leaves changed from green to yellow to brown. At first it was a treat for my eyes. But then the water iris dried up. The water lily pads wilted and disappeared under the surface. Summer heat gave way to chilling autumn winds that ripped the dead leaves from the trees and scattered them across the surface of the pond. The world grew drab.

Ducks and geese talked excitedly as they checked out their children's flight feathers. The fledglings were learning to fly. I swam by in feigned nonchalance, but really I watched every detail.

The fathers went off in their own groups, eating and socializing. But the mothers were busy at work. Mother musk ducks swam in quick circles, their neck lobes swinging in a cheerful way, till their young ran across the top of the water and finally took to the air. Mother Cape Barren geese made happy, high-pitched honks, higher than Honker and Grunter used to make, till their young did the same. It lifted my spirits to see those pretty goslings, with their black upper parts and broad white side-stripes. Flying adventures lay ahead of them. Adventures with their flocks.

What I watched most carefully, though, were the Pacific black ducks. Alert and wary, the mothers eyed me suspiciously, so I had to stay at a distance. But my long neck helped me get a good view anyway. The mothers gave encouraging quacks—four in a row, just like my own mother used to do.

And their young flew. They didn't run across the top of the water like the geese; instead, they rose straight into the air. It amazed me. How could they do that? My wings twitched with longing.

My own flight feathers were in, of course. Soon after leaving Old Woman's home, my down had begun falling out and my feathers had gradually come in. By the time I had reached the age of two months, I was ready to fly. But there was no one to teach me. And I was afraid to practice on my own in front of everyone. If the other ducks saw me, they'd realize that, despite my size, I was just a duckling. Then they might attack me. I couldn't risk being driven away from this pond. I didn't know where else to go.

So I did nothing but swim. Frustrated and miserable. I stopped watching the teals and musk ducks and geese. But I couldn't pull my eyes away from the Pacific black ducks.

Day by day the fledglings became stronger fliers. The Pacific black duck mothers went off to one end of the pond to molt, while the young joined their fathers. High-pitched quacks mixed with low, reedy queks—the young and their fathers together.

I hated hearing it—and at the same time, it was the only thing I wanted to hear.

It grew cold. Bitter. Some mornings there was ice at the edges of the pond.

Then the mothers came back and joined their families.

One morning soon after that, the ducks left. They simply took to the sky, forming their own cloud. I watched, silent. The youngest Pacific black ducks noisily leapfrogged each other in the air as they found their places in the flight pattern. The green glossy patches on the adult males' upper wings flashed with every flap. The white feathers of their underwings beckoned me.

Every part of me ached to spread my wings and follow. But I didn't know if I could fly. And what was the point in trying now? They'd only shun me. I wouldn't go through that. Not again. Never again.

The next day the geese left.

I knew where everyone was going. North, like Mother had said so long ago. North. The north country was full of ducks and geese. I was supposed to go north, too. But I couldn't face it without a flock.

I was totally alone now. No more quacks. No more honks.

At dusk the very next day, four huge birds landed on the pond announcing themselves with triumphant, majestic trumpeting. They had enormous wings, serpentine necks, deep orange-red bills with a white band near the tip. Their bodies were so deep brown they looked almost black. I had never seen anything so staggeringly gorgeous in my life. Not even Mother was as stunning as the two females. And the males captured my admiration totally. They were young, I could tell. They hadn't yet had clutches. But it was clear they had chosen mates. These were two pairs of lovers. And they didn't appear to have noticed me.

My heart thumped crazily. I couldn't think. I swam quickly toward the shore and hid. I spied on the couples through the tangle of dry, bare bushes at the lake's edge.

They fed voraciously, their sinuous necks disappearing underwater for a long time, then coming up with gobs of browning grasses. The couples swam past each other so close their feathers brushed. The slow strokes of their feet were synchronized. They dipped their bills in the water and blew bubbles toward each other. Everything about them showed their affection.

Then, in trumpeted agreement, all four ran across the top of the water, faster and faster till they finally took flight. They rose higher and flew faster than the ducks and geese. In flight I could see stark white at the very tips of their wings.

My feathers stood stiffly out, ready for flight. I wanted to follow. I loved those birds. It was absurd. Ridiculous, as Mother would have said. I was behaving like a much younger duckling. But I couldn't help it. I loved them. I wanted to be with them. Now and always.

Birds as gorgeous as those would never accept me, though.

And they were large enough to kill me if they wanted to.

I swam in circles in the icy water. I opened my mouth to quack my feelings of loss. Instead, the strangest sound came out of me. A kind of broken trumpet, as though I was giving a hideously poor imitation of the miraculously musical call of those grand birds.

How stupid, stupid, stupid of me. Wallaby and Wombat and Honker and Grunter and Pama Chick and Mapali Cat—all of them were right. I was stupid. I was nobody's darling genius. Those magnificent birds would hate me. I was nothing like them. I hated myself in that moment. I hated myself for being so ugly that I could never ever be with those birds.

I slept badly that night. Frigid winds blew. Even with my head under my right wing, I could hear their whine. The water was so cold I couldn't feel my feet.

In the morning ice had formed around me. I had to kick and throw myself about to get free. I slipped and slid over the ice to open water.

The next morning the ledge of ice around the edges of the pond was thicker and wider. Within a few days, there wasn't much open water left. I spent all my time swimming in circles just to keep the surface from freezing over entirely.

I swam and swam. I swam till I had no energy left.

Then, one night, I gave up.

When morning sun woke me, I was stuck fast in

ice. I struggled at first, but it made not the slightest difference. And I had no strength, anyway. I'd been so busy fighting to keep the water from freezing that I hadn't eaten anything for days. I stretched my neck and rested the bottom of my bill on the surface of the ice. There was nothing left to do. And I

was too cold and too exhausted to care. I closed my eyes.

Gradually the sense of cold left me. All I could feel was the weight of my own body. Existence had become heavy.

"What's this?" came a voice.

I opened one eye.

On the ice beside me stood a human being, much like Old Woman, only male and larger and with different coloring. "Looks like you need help.

I think I'll take you home with me. What do you say to that?"

Help. Friends helped each other. If I weren't so far gone, I'd want a friend. But, while home for creatures like him meant food and warmth, it also meant imprisonment.

I didn't move.

He kicked at the ice with the strange hard stuff that covered his feet. Then he banged at it with a rock. He broke me free, put an arm around my middle, and carried me away, my limp neck swinging before him.

He walked a long time, and he had a vigorous stride. Soon I could feel my blood moving again, though sluggishly. I shivered.

"Hey," called the human being, at last. He opened the door of a wooden house. "Hey, Wife."

We stepped into warm, fragrant air and the door banged shut behind us.

"What have you got there, Husband?" said Wife. She was fatter and younger than Old Woman. "A huge bird? Don't you know those things are dangerous?"

"This one seems pretty docile," said Husband.

Snow and ice melted off me in little puddles on the floor. All my parts were waking up again, and, oh, the pain of having nearly frozen almost made me pass out.

"Docile? Half-dead is more like it." Wife dried her hands on the stuff that covered her plump belly. "Children!"

Little versions of Husband and Wife came running through another door, across the cluttered room. Three of them, in different sizes.

"A bird!"

"I wish I was a bird."

"He's big. Let's ride him."

Husband set me on the floor in a wet heap.

"Wait just one minute," said Wife. "This bird's not in good shape. But once he's regained his strength, there's no telling what he'll do. See that bill there? It can bite."

"I'll bite him back. And pull his teeth out," raved the middle-size one.

I flinched and forced myself to stand, no matter how much it hurt. I probably couldn't win against this rabid human, but I wouldn't give up without a fight. For the moment I'd keep my bill shut, though.

Let them think I had teeth—it might hold them off a while.

"Look, you scared him. Bad boy. He's a good birdy. He's going to teach me how to fly." The littlest one ran in a circle flapping her puny arms. She was clearly a lunatic; she'd never take to flight.

"Don't be stupid," said the big one. "You can't fly in July. The winter sky would freeze you. Anyway, I'm the oldest. That bird's mine. He'll sleep in my bed and . . ."

"Hush," said Wife. "We'll feed him. Then we'll see what we'll do about him."

Meanwhile Husband had taken a seat at the table. "Now that sounds like a good idea for all of us. The pumpkin stew smells good."

Children took their places at the table. And just like that, I was no longer the center of attention. Still, I didn't dare move.

Wife ladled out food for her family.

She put some in a bowl and set it on the floor beside me. It smelled okay. I poked my bill in tentatively. It was hot. I'd never eaten hot food before. I nibbled at it. Slowly the savage chill in my bones eased. I ate and ate and ate.

Children watched me.

"Bird's still hungry."

"He needs more."

"Give him more, Mommy."

Wife didn't move. She didn't even look at me.

Husband looked over at me, though. He got up and refilled my bowl. I ate all that. Husband refilled it again. And again.

"That bird is going to eat us out of house and home," said Wife.

The children licked their bowls.

"It's time to play!"

"How about 'chase the bird'?"

"Yay!"

Children ran at me, laughing, their claws outstretched.

I fluttered up to a shelf in fright and knocked something over. White liquid cascaded down the wall.

"The milk pail! What a mess," said Wife. "Come down from there right now!" She clapped her hands angrily.

The noise rattled me so much, I lost my footing and landed in slippery stuff.

Children laughed and danced around the room.
"He's Butter Barrel Bird."
"He's Big Butter Barrel Bird."
"He's Big Bad Butter Barrel Bird."
They danced faster and faster and burst out in
song.

"Waltzing matilda, waltzing matilda
You'll come a waltzing matilda with me
And he sang as he watched and waited 'til his billy boiled
You'll come a-waltzing matilda with me."

"Out of there right now!" shouted Wife above
the din of the children's voices. She threw her arms
around me and lifted me out, squeezing hard.

So hard, I slipped free, and landed *splat* in
another barrel.

"He looks so funny, covered with butter and meal."
"Like potato cake."
"Let's fry him."

"Out!" shrieked Wife. She grabbed the fire
tongs and ran at me.

Children stretched their arms long and ran at
me, too, laughing and screaming.

I turned in a circle, too afraid of bashing into things to run. There was nowhere to go anyway. I was trapped.

Husband held the door open. "This way, Bird. This way."

I ran through that blessed door, out into the glare of sun on snow. I kept running, pumping my wings, bouncing higher and higher, running, running, and suddenly my feet were off the ground and hanging out behind me in the air, all loose and floppy. I was flying! Me! Flying at last!

It was phenomenally glorious. I beat the air with my wide wings. I soared high. Husband's home looked like a little pebble way down there. How funny. I swooped away and circled the mountainside.

The world was nothing but white snow beneath and blue sky above. It was quiet and peaceful up here. Empty. Wonderful. I felt I could fly forever.

And I did fly for hours.

But I had nowhere to go and no idea of what to do next.

Eventually, I landed.

Snow gave way beneath me. My feet hung free below the crusty surface now; my body was held up by leafless branches. I had landed on low, snow-covered shrubs. I wriggled my way down, letting my weight do most of the work, till I was completely inside the bushes. My feet touched the frozen ground and my body rested on my feet. I stretched my long neck up through the branches and poked my bill out through the snow far enough to breathe fresh air. Gradually, my body heat warmed up the little lair I'd found myself in.

My belly was full, I was warm and hidden. No tormentors knew where I was. For now, that was good enough. I could sleep in peace and dream of flying.

CHAPTER TEN

Found

WINTER was hard and long. I came to understand only too well why water birds left Tasmania for the mainland of Australia during these months. I searched for open water here in the mountains. I didn't find any. The only way to get a drink was to eat snow. It burned my tongue and throat and felt like a stone in my stomach.

I foraged pretty much all day long. Dried leaves and berries and even, occasionally, dormant gum beetles—I ate them all, gratefully. But there were far too few. Hunger became my normal state.

The only joy in my day was flying. But that was a superb joy.

I took to the air at midday and beat my wings hard. I circled high, craggy mountain peaks, and looked down over rock-strewn valleys so deep in snow that only the biggest boulders made bumps in the surface. I flapped over tall pines, and wide snow gums, and scrub trees that grew horizontally, so that their twisted branches looked like teeming snakes. I passed frozen waterfalls and glistening rivers of ice. Here in this mountainous area, I was king of the air. Up high where I flew, no one else dared go.

But the rest of the day was dismal. I was lost—there was no other way to describe it. And the night was worse—because the night was long and colder. I slept in snow lairs that I discovered under bushes and rock ledges.

Once I was lucky enough to come across a wombat tunnel. I could have laughed at my old vow to stay out of wombat burrows. Why, they were just the right size for my large body to snuggle into. I

backed in, ready to roll fast at the first sign of a spi-
derweb, and slept close to the entrance. For the
next several weeks, this was my sleeping quarters.
It wasn't warm, but it was out of the wind. The
wind was my worst enemy. It could suck the heat
from me in an instant.

Then one evening I returned to the tunnel from
a rather disappointing day of foraging, only to face
a confused but territorial wombat. He turned his
bottom to me and plugged up the entrance with it.
My blood raced. My neck bobbed up and down. I
was ready to fight for my home—oh, was I ready.
Fortunately, I remembered about the cartilage in
wombats' bottoms. Otherwise I might very well
have ended right then and there, my head crushed
against the tunnel wall.

I left, defeated. But now that I'd had the secure
shelter of a tunnel, I didn't want to go without it.
So I searched for another burrow. I searched all
night and all the next morning. I was so determined
to sleep wind-free that I left the area around my
frozen pond and flew down into a low valley. I followed the sound of water to a slow-moving, icy
river.

I landed on the bank and drank the frigid water. When I looked up, I saw the opening of a burrow just above the waterline on the other side of the river. It was too small to make a decent home, though. I was about to waddle on when the very next moment a bill stuck out of the hole. A duck bill.

Any duck without a flock had to be desperate with loneliness.

Company at last!

I jumped into the water and swam toward the new duck.

His webbed feet now emerged, sticking out on either side of his bill. How odd! I imagined him all scrunched up in that hole. I couldn't think of a more uncomfortable position.

Now his whole head appeared, a lovely deep brown.

I swam closer, neck extended. "Hello," I called. My voice cracked, I hadn't used it in so long.

The little duck slipped into the water and went under. But I got a quick glimpse of his streamlined body and flat tail and hind legs. Hind legs? My eyes couldn't have seen right.

I dipped my head underwater and gawked. The duck zipped along, that broad tail acting like a rudder. He seemed more like some sort of giant lizard than a duck. I swam after him, then put my head down again to get a closer look. But I came too close; I bumped into him.

Aiiii! Something sharp stabbed me on the side of my neck. I lifted my head out of the water and trumpeted in dismay.

The duck climbed out on the far bank and looked at me. "Serves you right."

The injustice of that got to me. "You're a bad duck," I said. He really was. My neck throbbed. It was all I could do to hold my head up. The memory of the many neck nips I endured in my week at Dove Lake came back like a sudden flame. I blurted out with rage, "And a dumb duck, too. Look how big I am. I ought to come over there and trounce you."

"Duck? Did you call me a duck?" The little creature growled. "I'm a platypus, you numskull." He stretched out a hind leg. "As for trouncing, see this spur on my leg? That's what I jabbed you with. You're lucky I didn't squirt poison into the wound.

If you mess with me, you won't be lucky again. Go
away, you big oaf. I'm hungry, and I like to be alone
when I feed." He shook the water off his back.

And now I could see that those weren't feathers
covering him, they were furry hairs. "You're a marsupial," I said in astonishment. "A marsupial with a
bill."

"Marsupials are common and boring. I am definitely not a marsupial."

"You have to be. You have fur. Mother told
me."

"Then your mother is as brainless as you."

I shook my chest feathers. "Mother knows everything. You're a marsupial."

"No, no, no. Stop insulting me. I'm a mono-treme. We're worlds different. Our females lay eggs."

"Like a duck," I blurted out, before I realized he'd take it as another insult.

"That's it!" growled the platypus. He dove into the river.

I didn't wait to see if he was coming after me. I ran across the top of the water and flew off, straight for the mountains again.

Monotremes were dangerous. That little beast had hurt me a lot.

And, worse, much much worse, Mother had been wrong about something.

What other dangers were lurking out there in this big world?

I didn't leave the mountains after that. I went back to foraging in the snow. And every night I made a sleeping lair by shoving my way under bushes or rock ledges.

Until the night twigs rained down on my head.

I had taken a
nap out in the
open, at the edge
of a stand of low
trees. Something
landed lightly on my
nose hole. I woke.
Something landed on
the other nose hole.
I blew my nose clear.
Bits of bark speckled the
moonlit snow around me.
I looked up.

Two yellow balls glowed
at me. I knew instantly that
they had to be eyes. They seemed
to float in space under a gum-tree
branch; I couldn't make out a body
below them.

I stood up warily.

"Click. Click. Click, click, click."

I stretched my neck tall and moved closer.

"Haaaa," came a long exhalation. "Haaaa."

Now I could see the open mouth below those

eyes. Tiny rows of sharp pearly teeth. And between the eyes and mouth was a pink nose with long whiskers that caught the moonlight when they twitched.

"Haaaa," threatened the disembodied head. Its big ears stood stiff in points. "Go away or I'll rip you to shreds. Haaaa."

"Haaaa, yourself," I hissed back. "You're nothing but a head."

"Deadbeat," said the head. "You've got junk for brains."

All my life I'd been called names. I was pretty good at letting insults roll off me. And after the platypus, I knew that the size of an opponent didn't matter; small things could inflict serious wounds. But here was a mere head abusing me. I was cold and hungry and lonely—and abuse from a head was too much to take. I jumped, ready to give that head a good smack with my bill.

The head swung to the side and I saw a glossy sheen of yellow-orange above it. Why, this creature's body was attached above its head, instead of below. How did that work?

I landed back on the snow and stared upward in

amazement. I walked around under the tree, looking at her from all angles, till I finally figured it out. "You're hanging from the tree branch by your back feet." I walked in front of her again. "And your back is to me, so your head is tilted all the way to the rear so you can see me."

"Aren't you the genius." It wasn't a question.

Mother called me a genius. Her darling genius. And this upside-down creature had now turned Mother's praise into garbage. I was popping with anger. I jumped, this time aiming my bill for the middle of her back.

The creature swung away again. She landed up on the tree branch and stood there, with her fore-limbs outstretched and raised, ready for battle. A musky odor invaded my nose holes. She let out a scream.

I could see her fairly clearly now. She was actually a small thing. In her haste to look and smell and sound ferocious, her exceedingly long and bushy tail had dropped below the branch. If I wanted, I could have easily caught it and pulled her down from there and given her a good thrashing.

The absurdity of this fluffy little gal trying to

scare big ugly me was too much. I couldn't stay mad. I let out a ragged laugh.

She stretched to full height and screamed louder.

I admired her spunk. "Your tail, " I said, pointing with my bill.

She quickly pulled her tail up and wrapped it several times around the branch. Then she got into a squat and leaned toward me. "I'm a powerful fighter," she said.

"I believe it," I said back.

"If you had pulled me down by my tail, I'd have made you sorry."

"I believe that, too," I said. "But not for the reason you think."

"What's that mean?"

"You're pretty," I said. "And you've got courage. I would have been sorry to hurt as pretty a warrior as you."

"I'm a Golden Brushtail Possum," she said. "Of course I'm pretty. I'm sensational. And all possums are brave."

Brave. If I had been brave, I'd have tried to follow the gorgeous birds that landed on the pond last autumn. "You're lucky," I said softly.

She looked at me thoughtfully. "What are you doing here? Don't birds like you go away in winter?"

"It's a long story," I said.

"The night is long, and I've already eaten. That's what woke you, I bet. I'm a messy eater."

"I'm a messy eater, too," I said.

"Oh, yeah? Well, anyway, I've got the time. Tell me the long story."

I told Possum the story of my life. Right from the beginning. By the time I finished, dawn was breaking over the mountain peak. She hadn't said a word as I talked. And now she still stayed silent. "Are you asleep?" I asked.

"I never sleep out in the open." Possum walked back and forth along the gum branch. Then she stopped and squatted and leaned toward me again. "All right, buddy, I don't really understand your loneliness. Being alone is good in my opinion. When I come across the scent of another possum, I generally change direction. We avoid each other. Unless it's mating time. Then we call each other like this. Ka-ka-ka-ka."

Her mating call came in loud, guttural, staccato

bursts. I didn't find it the least attractive. But I tried to keep a pleasant look on my face.

"Anyway, what I mean is, you're weird. But you seem like a decent sort. You didn't kill me, after all. And I have a feeling you could be of help."

Help? Was she asking for friendship? "I'm listening," I said.

"Well, you know how you kept climbing up on your mother's back . . . I was wondering, do you think you'd like to have a little one climb on your back?"

The idea was new, but my response was instantaneous. "I'd love it."

"Can you be patient?"

I didn't know if I'd ever had my patience tested. "Yes," I said optimistically. If patience didn't come naturally, I could learn it, I was sure. Any genius could.

"Then come with me. In another two months, I'll have something to show you. In the meantime, you can be patient."

I followed her to a nest in a hollow tree. I pressed in, fidgeted for a moment, then settled down. Possum followed, and immediately curled her body around mine. The surprise of feeling another warm body for the first time since I'd left Wombat made me gasp. "Your fur is really nice," I said.

"Don't go all mushy and sentimental on me." Possum wriggled a little to get comfortable. "This is going to be a business arrangement. Mutually beneficial. Sleep now."

I suppressed a happy sigh. I'd been found, by a decidedly odd creature, it was true—but being found was a zillion times better than being lost, no matter who found me.

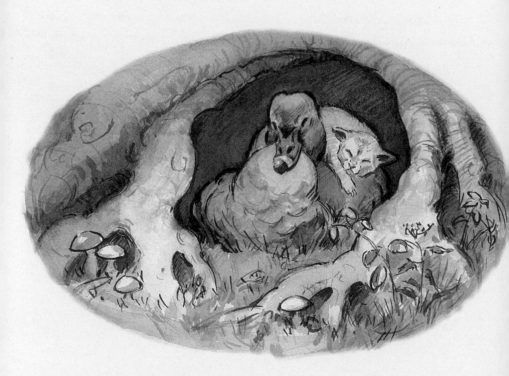

That tree became our home together. We got into a nice routine. We slept most of the day. Then at dusk we foraged together. I found food on the ground and she found food in the trees. We had similar tastes, so we shared. And we were both so hungry that we cleaned up each other's messes, swallowing every last bit.

Possum was a quick climber, but a clumsy one. Sometimes she'd skitter across branches too enthusiastically, and wind up splat on the snowy ground beside me.

She told me she'd once run across a human being's roof and fallen down his chimney by accident. When she described the inside of the house and the chaos that the three children inside had caused chasing her all around, I realized she was talking about Husband's house. We laughed over that.

We laughed over lots of things. Even when they weren't funny. It felt good to laugh. Good to talk, good to be understood.

Slowly over the next two months the world changed again. White turned to brown. Brown turned to green. Wildflowers peeked up everywhere. The daylight hours grew long. And best of all, the pond thawed. Soon I was back to gliding along, eating underwater grasses, while Possum scampered through the trees on the shore eating flowers and insects.

But when it came time to sleep, we still cozied up to each other in the hollow tree. That was the part of the day I looked forward to most of all.

CHAPTER ELEVEN

The Cob

ONE LATE afternoon, I woke staring into two sets of yellow glowing eyes—Possum's, that I knew so well—and new ones. Teeny-weenie ones. They were on a teeny-weenie head that stuck out of Possum's pouch.

"You're a mother," I said, stupefied. "Congratulations."

"I've been a mother for the past five months," said Possum. "But my baby hid in my pouch. Now he's ready to come out and ride on my back."

I watched as the baby crawled out of Possum's pouch. He was the spitting image of her, only miniature. He climbed around to Possum's back and looked at me over Possum's shoulder.

"He's perfect," I breathed in awe.

"That's a good name for him," said Possum. "Perfect, meet your uncle."

"Hi, Uncle," said Perfect.

"Pleased to meet you, Perfect," I said.

"Now you can be of help," said Possum.

"What do you mean? We've been helping each other all along," I said. "We share when we forage."

"Foraging is easy now that the snow's gone. What I need help with is watching Perfect. Possums aren't the most graceful creatures, as you know by now. And I have a taste for leaves and flowers from the very tops of trees. I don't know why. I just do. I don't want Perfect to get hurt if I fall. So when I need to go high, Perfect can stay with you."

The light dawned. "On my back, you mean? Yes!" That's when the real fun started. Possum ran through the treetops and I waddled along on the ground, with Perfect tucked neatly inside my back feathers. Only his little head showed. He looked out at the world happily. At first I waddled extra slowly, picking my way carefully over tree roots and rocks. But Perfect held on tight, and soon I was waddling faster and faster.

It was time for me to begin Perfect's education.

"I'm going to teach you everything," I said to Perfect. "Rule number one: Don't get eaten."

"Okay," said Perfect.

He was such a smart little fellow. He learned fast. I swung my long neck around and nuzzled Perfect. "Rule number two: Never attack another duck unless."

"Okay," said Perfect.

But now that I thought about it, I didn't even like that rule. And, as I had learned when I got spurred by the platypus, Mother wasn't always right.

I wanted to do my best by Perfect. He deserved nothing less. So it was time to think for myself.

Maybe that's even what Mother wanted when she told me to use my head. Her final parting gift.

"I take that rule back," I said, walking very firmly, to show my decisiveness.

"Okay," said Perfect.

What a flexible little fellow. Oh, he was aptly named, if I do say so myself. "Rule number two— that is, new rule number two: Stay close."

"Okay," said Perfect. And suddenly he was moving around under my back feathers in a fury.

"What are you doing?" I asked.

"Rubbing." The flurry of activity continued.

I swung my neck around again and parted my

feathers with my bill. Perfect was rolling around rubbing his throat all over me. "Why?"

"I'm practicing. When I get big, I'll mark my territory with my scent glands."

Oh. That meant I was Perfect's territory. Oh. It was a great responsibility to be someone's territory. And I was up to it. I strutted now. "Rule number three: Eat greens."

"What about fruits?" said Perfect.

"Fruits? Well, certainly, eat fruits, too."

"Okay," said Perfect.

I was flustered now. Perfect's question had shown me I might not know the best way for a pos- sum to face the world. Well, there were really only two rules left, and I didn't see how either of them could harm him. "Always be ready to dash. And never eat a log."

"Okay, okay," said Perfect.

Good, that was over. We spent the rest of our time just enjoying each other.

Perfect showed such good balance and ability to hold on no matter what happened, that within a week I had the confidence to take him on the pond with me. I ripped up underwater grasses and tossed a few over my shoulder. Perfect held them in his paws and nibbled daintily. He was an altogether pleasant and comforting companion.

He grew fast. By the end of a month his fur had fluffed out all puffy and long. Possum combed it with her sharp claws and I smoothed it with my bill. What a fine little fellow Perfect was.

One spring dawn I was gliding through the cool water with Perfect on my back when I heard the whine of wings in flight. We'd been foraging most of the night and I was fairly sleepy, so at first I thought it was my imagination. But then I heard the calls. My skin prickled into little bumps. It was them. The sound was unmistakable. Powerful, musical trumpets. A large flock of the giant birds that I loved landed in noisy profusion on the pond.

My head spun. I was out in the open. I could hear Mother's voice inside me, telling me to dash for cover. But it was too late to hide. And I realized that I didn't want to hide this time, anyway. The feeling that I belonged with those birds over-whelmed me. I had to be with them. This is what thinking for myself meant. This was my moment of truth.

"Hang on tight, Perfect," I said over my shoulder. "If you get worried, just bury yourself in my feathers." I swam toward the flock.

The whole flock jerked their heads up in instant alarm. A huge male bobbed his head up and down. He cocked his elbows, stretched his neck out low, and made a threatening, raucous hiss. "Beat it," he said.

I stopped short. It was my ugliness, ruining everything again. Always. I wouldn't let it. Not this time. "I may be an ugly duck," I said. "But I'm a genius. And I know how to be a good friend. I can help. Just let me into your colony and I'll prove it."

"A berserk cob," screamed the male. He rushed at me.

"Don't!" I shouted. "You'll hurt the baby." I cocked my own wings and let out a loud bugle. If I had to, I'd fight this male. I'd protect Perfect to the death.

The male stopped midway in the water. "Baby? Where?"

Perfect peeked out around my neck. "Hi," he called.

The male's bill dropped open.

"Hi," Perfect called to all the other birds in the flock.

They stared at him. Then one young female blinked her eyes and called back, "Hi." Her face showed she thought he was dear. Darling, in fact.

My blood rushed. I wanted her to look at me like she looked at Perfect. But she turned away.

The male glided toward me, his eyes watchful but no longer hostile. "Are you crazy?"

"No," I said.

"That's a possum baby on your back."

"I know. I'm a good friend to his mother. See? I can be useful, even if I am an ugly duck."

"I'm Handsome Cob," he said. He glided around me slowly. "You're a year old. Young—but not young enough to excuse this mistake. I don't know who told you you were a genius, but you're definitely a blockhead if you think you're a duck."

What was he talking about? "My mother was a Pacific black duck. My father was a Pacific black duck."

"Someone sure pulled a good one over on them then. Look at that fellow there." He pointed with his bill.

I looked. Among the dark birds was a young male the same gray-brown color as me.

"Now look in the water," said Handsome Cob.

I bent my head down. My reflection in the water startled me. I used to look at it all the time when I was a babe. I used to wish for the shape and size and coloring of my siblings. But I hadn't looked at it for a long time now. I stared. I couldn't believe my eyes. I looked at the young male again to be sure.

Same dark bill. Same long neck. Same colors everywhere. "I look just like him," I said to Handsome Cob in bewilderment.

"Surprise, surprise. Still think you're a duck?"

"What am I?"

"An Australian black swan. A cob, like me. In another year, your feathers will change. All the two-year-olds' feathers will change. You'll all be glorious black. And your bill will turn red."

I loved those words. I was an Australian black swan. I was a cob. This shape and size and coloring—this was what I was meant to have. "Then I'm not ugly?"

Handsome Cob held his head high. "Definitely not. In fact, you look very much like I did as a

youngster." He glided off. "Follow me. I'll introduce you around."

I followed eagerly.

"Hi," called Perfect to everyone we met. 'Hi, hi,
hi."

We swam past the young male, who nodded
just slightly. He seemed like a good fellow, even if
a bit reserved.

Near him were two more young gray-brown
swans. One was the female who had answered
Perfect before. Her eyes met mine. She blinked.
Then looked away. Then looked back and blinked
again.

I was completely charmed. I just bet she was
kind and wise.

"Yoo-hoo," called Handsome Cob. "Do you
want to meet everyone or not?"

I swam fast after him.

"That little pen you were just making eyes at is
my daughter."

"She's marvelous," I said.

"Indeed."

"Your whole colony is completely wonderful," I
said. "Swans are wonderful."

"So you've spent this past year in a flock of ducks?"

"No," I said. "The ducks buffeted me. I spent this past year here. Cold."

The cob watched me thoughtfully.

"Alone," I added.

"Alone." Handsome Cob winced. "That's hard for anyone. But if you want to join us, I'm afraid you'll have to leave this pond."

Leave the pond?

That meant leave Possum and Perfect.

I'd grown attached to them. Very.

But in another month, Perfect would be completely independent. Possum wouldn't need me anymore. They'd both go off. They'd both leave me.

So if Possum could just stay out of the treetops for one month, Perfect would be fine. Without me.

I'd miss them.

I looked over my shoulder at Perfect.

His intelligent little eyes stayed steadfastly on me. They were sad. But he lifted his chin with a bravery his mother would have been proud of. He didn't have to say anything; I knew he understood.

"Okay," I whispered, mimicking him.

"We breed at Dove Lake," said Handsome Cob.
"Ever heard of it?"

Dove Lake. My true home.

"Well?" said Handsome Cob.

I let out a happy trumpet.

CHAPTER TWELVE

Dove Lake

I MET Possum back at our hollow tree. It was time to sleep. My last day sleeping with her and Perfect. I figured I'd break the news when we woke up.

But the instant Perfect saw Possum, he jumped from my back to hers and blurted out, "Uncle's going."

Possum's pink nose twitched. She looked at me.

Perfect climbed around to Possum's tummy.

"With big birds just like him." He disappeared into Possum's pouch to nurse.

"I'm a swan," I said. "An Australian black swan."

"Good for you," said Possum.

"You and Perfect are dear to me. I'm so sorry, but . . ."

"Don't go all mushy on me," said Possum. She lay on her side and curled her tail around her. "I told you, this was a business arrangement. No sentimentality. You did your job well. Thanks."

"Thank you, too. I'll miss you."

"It's time for Perfect to learn how to make his own way through the trees. Yes, this happened at just the right time."

"I'll miss you."

"It's right for you to be with birds just like you. All of this is exactly right."

"I said, I'll miss you." I stood over Possum and put my head down close to hers. "And I'll miss Perfect."

Possum made a little guttural sound.

"Won't you miss me?" I asked.

Possum's nose twitched again. "You had to leave

sooner or later. Once mating season starts, whatever male possums come after me would have ripped you to shreds."

I was pretty sure I could fend for myself against a male possum. But I didn't want to argue. Not now. Not on our last day together. I cozied up against Possum.

"Stop right there," said Possum. "Where are those birds now?"

"Out on the water. Sleeping."

"Then go sleep with them." Possum's nose twitched. "Get out of here."

"There's no rush," I said. "They're not leaving till tonight."

"You belong with them." Possum's nose twitched. "Go on, get out of here." She closed her eyes.

The whole length of my long neck ached with a mixture of sadness and hope. I took one final look at Possum.

She opened an eye. "We'll miss you, too. Go be happy now." She closed her eye and her breathing told me she was already asleep.

I spent the rest of the day napping in the midst

of my new swan colony. The one-year-olds stayed near their parents. Even some of the two-year-olds did that. They were close families.

I didn't have a family, of course. But Handsome Cob let me sleep with his family. And Marvelous, the shy young pen I found so enchanting, floated along at my side, her neck arched in the most pleasing loop I'd ever seen. Her feathers curled the smallest bit. Completely captivating.

That night we raced across the water in preparation for taking to the air. Flying had been my solace through the long winter months alone. But during my time with Possum, I had hardly flown at all. So I looked forward to the thrill again.

Nothing could have prepared me, though, for the immediate and total exhilaration of night flying with a lamentation of swans—my lamentation. That's what a flock of swans were called: a lamentation. Handsome Cob had taught me. We stayed single file most of the time, our wings flapping in a natural and comforting harmony. Beat, beat, beat, strong against the current of the air.

Handsome Cob took the lead. He let out a clang whenever someone would lag too far behind. The rest of us were noisy, too, trumpeting for the simple pleasure of it.

We stayed high and flew fast for hours. There were mountains and forests below. Yet at times it seemed there was nothing. Only air all around, and clouds and stars and that wonderful lemon moon.

Then the air changed. It grew wetter. And the smell, oh, I knew that smell. I looked down. Sure enough, double peaks reached up toward us from

below. Cradle Mountain. A moment later Handsome Cob started the descent, to Dove Lake. Home, at last.

I was already overwhelmed with emotion when the most extraordinary thing happened. Marvelous caught up on my right, and our wings flapped in unison, the two of us as one. We landed in the water at the exact same moment.

All of us ate, exhausted but happy. It was so good to be here. We ate till we were stuffed.

"In a couple of days we can start mating," said Handsome Cob.

This was news. "All of us?" I said in surprise.

"Of course not," said Handsome Cob. "You youngsters will go off to the molting spot and stay there till the rest of us join you."

"How long will that be?"

"Well, first the pens have to lay the eggs. Then we build reed nests around them. Then we sit on them. Then we take care of the cygnets. It adds up. I'd say you won't see us again till late summer."

I didn't like the idea of losing my family group so soon. And for so long. But this is what it meant to be a swan. I could adjust. Especially if we were all together the rest of the year.

As morning came, we grouped into families to sleep. Marvelous glided slowly beside me. "All this food." She looked around admiringly. "This really is the best lake in the world."

I'd heard those words before. From Mother.

My mother.

When everyone else snoozed, I swam off by myself. This part of the lake was foreign to me. I stayed close to the shore, uncertain which way to go. I passed lots of ducks, of varying species. They moved out of the way at the sight of me. And I gave them wide berth. None were the kind of duck I was seeking.

In the late morning, I recognized a sand spit. I swam faster.

Squawk!

A duck flapped out from under the overhanging branches in front of me. A Pacific black duck. She dashed in a panic up onto the beach. A drake met her. They ran off together, quacking loudly.

I didn't recognize them.

But, oh, beyond them, was another female Pacific black duck. A very familiar one. She sat on a nest.

I swam toward her.

She turned her head and leveled one frightened eye on me.

I stopped, put my head underwater, and grazed slowly. When I lifted my head, the water around me was littered with the greens I'd ripped off. The mother duck sat tensely on the nest. Eyeing me. She hadn't budged. She wouldn't abandon those eggs no matter what.

I swam closer. "You're still a perfectly good mother, I see. As beautiful and wise and kind as ever."

She gasped. Her head rocked from side to side on her short neck as she examined me. "You still have magnificent lungs, I see. And only a genius could have survived all this time on his own."

From behind a rhododendron bush waddled out a young female duck. She hesitated and blinked at me. "Ugly?"

"It's good to see you, Blinky."

"You've changed."

"He grew up," said Mother. "Like you did. He's a swan."

"A swan?" Blinky blinked at me. "That freckled

duck was right. The last egg didn't hold a Pacific black duck, after all."

"But she was wrong about everything else." Mother looked at me. "A sweet egg hatched a sweet bird."

"Thank you," I said.

"And a handsome one, too," said Blinky. "No matter which way you look at him."

"Thank you."

"Well, then," said Mother, "I guess that's that. Go live a good swan life."

I paddled away slowly. Then I turned around.

"I could come by now and then. If you let me, I'll take your new ducklings for a ride on my back."

Mother rose up at the idea. Then she settled down again. "I'd like that."

"Good-bye," called Blinky.

I looked over my shoulder once, then glided toward the other end of Dove Lake, where Marvelous was waiting for me. Mother's last bit of advice reverberated in my chest. Yes, that's exactly what I'd do, what I was always meant to do: live a good swan life.

DEC 2 1 2005

DEMCO